MOLLY

I0630740

ALICE VL

2
Molly

Alice VL

3

Molly

Alice VL

4
Molly

CONTENTS

Alice VL

6
Molly

DEDICATION

My Darling,

When I am so absorbed in my world of make believe, you step back into the shadows and let me live there for a while.

When I come home to you, you console me when I say goodbye to my stories and characters.

Without you, I never want to return.

Alice VL

8
Molly

BROKEN

"No daddy! I don't want to go! You can't make me go!" Molly shouted through her tears as she held on to her father, while desperately pleading with him. James Starkey was a tall and sturdy man, and for most of her seventeen years, Molly had secretly feared him. She was taught early on that, as his daughter, she had no voice when it came to questioning the decisions her father had made. Molly was raised to obey and accept that his decisions were an unbroken rule in their family home, one that they had no right, or place to question.

Even though Molly was raised in a secure and loving home, James Starkey was a strict disciplinarian and it in no way occurred to her, or even crossed her mind to become rebellious, or act out in disobedience towards her father. Arguing, or violating his rules in any way, was never an option for Molly. Being the eldest of three children, she realized early on that she was the apple of her father's eye. She thought herself to be the luckiest girl in the entire world to boast with a father who loved her as unconditionally as he did, even though there were times Molly felt he could loosen up a little more around his family. She would often find herself staring at her father, and lightheartedly relate to him as a colonel in the army. She, along with her younger brother and sister secretly gave him the nickname, 'The Major,' and would in jest mimic him when he was out of hearing distance. At times, she felt that he was immensely unreasonable, but Molly rarely doubted his astuteness and wholeheartedly accepted his rules, while trusting him, and the decisions he had resolved to on their behalf unreservedly. Until that moment, his authority enhanced her feelings of safety and fortification, but in an instant, Molly questioned all she thought she knew about her father.

"Daddy, please!" She was frantically trying to change her father's mind, while desperate that somehow, he would revisit his decision, if only just once. In a single moment, she hardly cared that she was questioning him, and she worried even less that he might become irate with her. It had been only fifteen minutes earlier that he had informed the entire family that they were relocating to another town, leaving her much-loved Harper Valley permanently behind.

For the first time in her life, Molly felt insecure and desperately frightened. She adored her hometown, the town she was born into, the town that had raised her, and brought her beloved Ryan to her. She, along with her brother, Tyron and her sister, Megan, were born in Harper Valley, and had lived there in bliss, their entire lives. In an instant, her father was sternly informing the family that they were to leave their little coastal hometown, and move inland, to the city.

For Molly, the thought of leaving it all behind, was too much for her to bear. She was not prepared for the sudden changes that were about to come into her life, and she could by no means imagine living elsewhere. She loathed the city, and she knew her father well enough to know that he found the city insufferable. Nothing made sense to her, and she could in no way at all, understand why he had made such a drastic decision in such a short time, without any forewarning or any hint of the prospect that they may soon have to leave their hometown. She felt as though she was trapped in the core of a nightmare, and regardless of how frantic she attempted to fight his decision, or wrestle with him, she was powerless to awaken from her nightmarish reality.

'I can't leave here, I just can't!' She thought again and again while listening to her father as he quickly discussed the intended move with her mother, Sue. Although Molly's bond with her father had been stronger than the connection she shared with her mother, she knew that she could rely on her mother to stand by her when James became irrational from time to time. Sue was entirely devoted to her children, but she knew and accepted right from the start of their marriage, that James was the head of their home. Her opinions vastly differed from him from time to time, but she stood firmly by him, and was confident that he knew what paramount for their family was.

"Mommy, please! Talk to daddy, let me stay here!" Molly shouted out again while clenching her mother's hand. "Honey…" Sue glanced at her daughter, unsure of how to respond to Molly's pleading. She was instantly aware of the tears that had settled into her own eyes, while convinced that at that exact point in their lives, Molly's father had no other alternative, making the only decision that was fitting for them as a family.

Sue adored James and their three children, but she was abundantly aware that the move would be rigid on her family, and especially tough on Molly. "I can go and live at Ryan's! Or at Ida's house. I only have what's left of this year and next year before school draws to an end for me. Please, mommy. Daddy, please!" Molly was unrelenting as she frantically beseeched her parents.

For the first time in his life, James felt tremendous strain as he faced his daughter. He was copiously aware of the reality that taking his family away, would wreck not only Molly, but the family as a whole. He moved around to the kitchen table, and reluctantly sat down, and held the weight of his head in his hands. Molly made her way over to him and stood quietly behind her father. She had only moments earlier placed her hands gently on his shoulders when she discovered how challenging a time it was for him too. As much compassion as she felt for him, she had no penchant to surrender her dispute with him just yet. "Daddy, please! I don't want to leave, please let me stay." She pleaded with him for a second time, while trying her utmost not to cry.

James peered up at his daughter, agonizingly aware of the brokenness in her voice while trying to face her courageously. He pulled her down onto his lap, as he did so many times before when she was no more than a little girl. As he sat gazing at her, Molly was alerted to the sorrow in his own eyes. It seemed to Molly as though he had aged ten years in fifteen minutes, and it unexpectedly disturbed her. It was at that dreadful moment that she realized that moving his family away from Harper Valley, was as severe for him, as it was for her. She instinctively knew that her father's decision was one made out of extreme desperation. "Daddy, please let me stay here." Molly spoke tenderly while praying silently that he would feel some empathy for her, and permit Molly to remain behind in Harper Valley.

Molly had known Ryan since the day she was born. She often heard their parents converse and reflect back on the day they had met. Molly and Ryan were born on the same day in the same hospital, and less than ten minutes apart. While in labor, Sue and Maria had met for the first time and became firm friends when they discovered that they both relished at becoming mothers for what seemed equally daunting to both women. As they grew closer to one another, James and Joe developed a close friendship too. Molly and Ryan had become playmates and in due course, as the years passed by, and without any one person taking notice, they developed a relationship that began with a childlike friendship. A relationship that grew into a romance that left no room for anyone else. Molly was totally dedicated to Ryan and he in turn, was totally besotted with her. They spent every waking moment together, and occasionally at night, Ryan would creep into her childhood home, and sit in the corner of her bedroom, while he watched Molly sleep. Ryan was terrified of losing her, and obsessed about it virtually every day, even as a little boy.

When Molly became ill from time to time, Ryan refused to leave her side, and sat in close proximity of her while he told her stories of how he would take care of her when they were old enough. He would frequently catch up on her homework when she was off school, for the fear that she might fall behind, which in turn, would leave her a year behind him. They were often teased at school for acting like an ageing wedded duo. Ryan was never fascinated by any other girl, and Molly by no means looked twice at a different boy. For the duration of their lunch breaks at school, Ryan and Molly would sit away from the other children, designing their later life as one. Habitually, their friends would be amused by them, although it never seemed to disturb either Ryan or Molly. Ryan was keen to study abroad after he graduated from high school, while Molly was ready to give up all to follow him, just to remain close to him.

For James, it was repeatedly intricate to witness their relationship amplify at the pace it was escalating, but he accepted that it was merely typical for his daughter and Ryan to develop such a profound and private relationship at an incredibly young age. He frequently became anxious at the physically powerful force of their relationship, but he once more accepted early on that there was nothing he could do to slow them down. He once told Sue that it would be cruel to try and keep them apart, and he would constantly pray that they would encompass one another to rely and depend upon, at all times. James realized from the very beginning that Molly's entire existence revolved around Ryan, and he couldn't help but wonder what would eventually come to pass with his daughter, should anything ever separate them. He treasured his daughter and he wanted more than anything for her to be content. He was convinced that he would do all he could to enable the reality of her dreams, and that no sacrifice would be too great to witness Molly blissfully happy. Only in that instant, while he was listening to her imploring him to allow her to stay behind, James was only too aware that he adored his daughter, and he could barely begin to visualize parting with her as they left her behind. He was only too conscious of the loss she would endure by leaving Ryan behind, but James was more troubled with the overwhelming loss he and Sue would suffer, should they allow Molly to stay behind without them, in Harper Valley.

When he glanced at Molly yet again, James was certain that nothing could ever wound him more, and that he could never again be sadder, than he was at that very moment; the moment he realized that Molly could in no way at all, subsist without Ryan. Above all else, he could scarcely imagine life without his daughter, living safely and shielded under the same roof as he. She hadn't spent one day apart from Ryan since the moment they had entered the world together, and he was disturbed by the reality of how she would get by without him. She barely made friends, but moreover, it was alarming when he realized that he could count her friends on one hand. He remained still while staring at her and thought back to the day he questioned her with reference as to why she never made new friends. Her reply was simple; she had Ryan, and she was relatively happy to have him as her best and only friend. Other than Ida, Ryan was the one person that she turned to while she proudly introduced him as her closest friend. If Molly, by chance wasn't hanging out with him at his home, or if they weren't together on the beach, Ryan was more than likely at home with her. The Starkey's thought highly of Ryan, and unsurprisingly embraced him as a fraction of their family. James had been exceedingly fond of Ryan and surreptitiously approved of the fact that his daughter had fallen in love with someone like him. He absolutely trusted Ryan, and barely worried about her when they were out together. He too, frequently felt that their relationship had intensified far too rapidly, but at the same time, he knew that there was nothing he could do to impede their union.

James recalled the day that Molly had been rushed to the hospital for an emergency appendicitis procedure. Ryan was beside himself with worry, and unrelentingly pleaded with Maria to take him to her. James recalled that throughout her stay, Ryan refused to leave her even for a moment, compelling Maria to allow him to stay with her until she was discharged. When James and Sue arrived at the hospital in the mornings, they would constantly find Ryan on the bed beside Molly with a protective arm around her. For Molly, making decisions without Ryan's approval was tougher for her than she would like to disclose. At night, they would meet up at the pool and squander hours while caught up in conversation, when they thought that nobody knew.

Molly

James would watch them giggle and embrace through his bedroom window, and although it was thorny for him to witness how greatly his daughter depended on someone other than him, he was delighted that it was Ryan, and he was thankful that Ryan was constantly present for her.

He often turned away from them, perceptive of the fact that there would in no way ever, be anyone else who cherished his daughter in the manner that Ryan did. James knew that their relationship was more intimate than he approved of, but he accepted months ago that there was not anything he could do to try and slow them down. He raised his children to be fearless in expressing and receiving affection, but ideally, he would have preferred it if Molly was a fraction older. James watched them when they thought that no-one was looking, and he couldn't help but feel the distance breed between him and Molly. He was constantly aware of how diverse they looked on the outside, yet how parallel they were on the inside.

Molly was a petite young lady with long blonde hair and striking green eyes, where Ryan on the other hand, was taller. He was set apart with raven black hair, and eyes that seemed to be even darker at times, which he inherited from his Spanish parents. They were a striking couple, yet they were entirely oblivious of how beautiful they were to the outside world. Tyron and Megan were utterly dissimilar to Molly, and James couldn't help but feel a little left behind in her life. He was overwhelmed by the fact that Ryan was the most significant person in her life, and at times, he felt that at the very least and for the first couple of years of her life, he should have been the center of his daughter's life, her first love.

"Molly, you can't stay here. What about us?" He took his daughter into his arms and held her firmly against him while hoping that she could sense the anguish he felt within. Without responding to him, Molly buried her head in his chest, and sobbed so deafeningly that Sue was forced to take Tyron and Megan and lead them away from of the kitchen. "Daddy, please, I'm begging you." Molly pleaded softly through her tears. "My girl, I can't leave you here. I can't leave you behind and carry on with my life somewhere else, without you. You are still my daughter, Molly, and you are still under my roof. I promise you that if you don't fight this, if you don't wrestle with me, I will let you come back once you've graduated from high school." He made a valiant effort to offer his daughter a compromise, confident that he could barely even consider, leaving his sweetheart Molly behind.

Molly was still weeping when she reluctantly accepted that, regardless of how profoundly she pleaded and begged her

Alice VL

father, he would never have a change of heart. When James Starkey made a decision, there was no turning back. A decision was made, and this time would be no different to any other moment in time. She was wholly unaware of how misplaced her father would be without her, and she was convinced that he was self-interested and malicious. Molly pulled away from him, and abruptly felt hatred and anger build up inside of her for her father.

"You, dad, you are ruining my life! I hate you! I hate you!" She shouted out loud before she ran from the kitchen, and into the night. When James could no longer see her, he was sure that his daughter was escaping to Ryan. He allowed her to seek solace in his arms while she was angry, sensitive to the fact that he had shattered her heart.

Molly walked slowly up the path of the Neves home, alert to the suggestion that it would be one of the last times she would stroll up this path. It was a path that she was immensely familiar with. It made her feel safe each time she glanced up at their home. When she gazed down at her wristwatch, she was staggered to find that it was just after eight the evening. Molly had no desire for the rest of the Neves family to recognize that she was there to see Ryan. She unnoticeably walked around to his bedroom and was relieved to find that his bedroom light still burning. She knocked delicately on his window, while she tried dabbing at the tears that were lying wet on her cheeks. "Molly? What are you doing here? What's wrong? Have you been crying?" Ryan was nervous the moment he saw her, and quietly climbed out of his bedroom window to get closer to her. Ryan had never seen Molly cry, and it frightened him to consider the very notion that there may be something critically in the wrong with her. Molly turned away from him and made her way around to their swimming pool. He caught up with her, and took her into his arms, holding her securely against him. He remained silent while sensing that she was desperately unable to find the words to clarify why she had become so utterly dejected. In all the years that he had known Molly, he could scarcely reflect on even one day that she was so entirely despondent. It terrified him to witness her in such a state, and he knew that something awful had taken place only moments earlier. He wiped the tears from her eyes before he held her in his arms once more.

"Molly, you're scaring me?" He whispered hoarsely when he felt panic grip a hold of his heart. "Ryan …" Was all she was able to say before the tears began rushing down her cheeks yet again. "What happened?" He gently brushed her hair from her eyes. She gazed up into his eyes, unsure of what to say to him, or precisely how to tell him what she herself could barely understand. She noticed that his hair was tousled, and to her, the very sight of him reminded her of how enormously eye-catching he was. She smiled when she realized how utterly perfect he was for her, but at the same time, Molly wondered if she would ever feel better again. She treasured the fact that they appeared entirely diverse to one another, yet she was the girl that Ryan had chosen, the only girl that claimed his heart.

"We're leaving, Harper Valley." Molly lowered her head, unable to look him in the eye. While listening to herself telling Ryan that they were about to leave Harper Valley, she could not bear hearing her own voice tell her how valid, and excruciatingly final it was. Ryan stared at her in total disbelief, and the astonishment on his face was excruciating for her. Molly was instantly aware of the uncertainty in his voice and could barely consider a life without him. "What do you mean? You're moving?" Ryan placed his hands on her shoulders. He could barely comprehend all she was telling him, but he was certain, into the very core of him, that they were about to drastically transform and alter their lives significantly. Molly nodded while permitting her tears to flow freely all over again, and without saying a great deal of anything else.

"You can't! Why? You've lived here all your life. I don't understand? When did this happen? Where are you going?" Molly swallowed with great intricacy. She took Ryan's hands into her own, "Dad told us at dinner this evening. I don't want to go, Ryan, I don't want to leave you! I don't want to go to the city!" She was desperate for it all to vanish, and to preserve her life unerringly as it was, and just as it was that very morning, when she awoke.

Ryan turned away from her. Molly was positive that he was fraught with what all was happening, out of the blue. She was not the only one affected by the revelation. Ryan too, was finding it tricky to understand. He was under immense pressure to make sense of what Molly was saying, and it frightened him to consider a reality in which James was taking her away from him. It was a thought he could not envisage. An idea that swore to him that their lives would by no means at all, be as it once was. "You can stay here, Molly, with me? At our house." Molly gazed up at Ryan, and tenderly touched his face. "Dad won't let me. I tried." "He said I can come back when, when I've graduated from high school "When is that going to be? I'm never going to see you again." Once again, Molly was perceptive to the despair and desperation in his voice.

"I can visit you during holidays, Ryan?" "When are you leaving?" Molly was conscious of the fact that Ryan's heart had shattered, while she persuaded herself that she would never be the same again, after her leaving. "Next week." She bowed her head, unwilling and unable to face him. Ryan summarily and without warning, became livid at once. "What? Already? I'll talk to him. Let me talk to him," He began to stutter before Molly interrupted him. "I've tried, Ryan. He won't listen to me! You know how stubborn my father is." Ryan moved over to where they had spent countless of nights laying on the grass counting the stars. When he sat down gradually, Molly knew that their lives were about to transform forever. She bent down and kissed him tenderly. He responded by holding onto her as though to tell her that he would never let her leave. "I love you, Molly, but I'm going to lose you. I can feel it, don't let it happen to us." He whispered gruffly while laying her down on the grass. He gazed into her eyes, fraught to find traces of anything her eyes would promise him, that she would never leave his life. "I love you more, Ryan, and I'll find my way back to you, I promise. I'll never walk away from you. I will never say goodbye to you, and I will never, ever let go." She whispered softly as he undressed her, bit by bit.

They had made love under the stars time and again, but tonight Molly felt poles apart from any other night. She had a niggling sensation that their lives would on no account, be the same again after that night. She was frantic to take in all about him, all about how he made her feel, afraid that not too far from that very moment, she might not remember any of the little details. She was desperately afraid that she might lose sight of what they once shared. She closed her eyes and felt his body against hers. Being with Ryan was unerringly where she yearned to be, eternally. Ryan felt his stomach turn while he made love to her. He, too, made a courageous effort to memorize all about her. He was frenetic to hold on to her and he prayed that the night would never end.

Molly held firmly onto Ryan for a long while after they had made love. Molly found herself wishing on each star she could see, and that somehow, they would wake up from their nightmarish ordeal in the morning. She wished that their lives would remain precisely as they were for the past seventeen years. They could take her away from Ryan, they could place distance and time between them, but her heart would ceaselessly remain behind with Ryan. Her heart was in no way at all, equipped to let him go.

Ryan walked Molly home in silence, and when he said goodbye to her, he was once again aware of a familiar sense of terror and fear tugging at his heart. He could almost predict that life as they knew it was about to alter, and that there was nothing he could do to make it remain unchanged, faithfully, and exactly as it were until then. The option to allow Molly to stay behind, rested exclusively and absolutely with James Starkey, but Ryan

Molly

knew that James was not ready to surrender her up to him just yet. Ryan tried to remain constructive and optimistic. He did his best to trust the love he and Molly shared for one another, but he could hardly shake the feeling that it was all about to come to an abrupt end for them.

Alice VL

THE PROMISE

The Neves family accompanied Molly and the rest of the Starkey family to the airport on the morning of their departure to Park Hill. Sue and Maria found it complex to say goodbye, but James swore to Joe that they would visit regularly. They had been the greatest of friends for the past seventeen years, and even though James knew that they were all reluctant, yet compelled to leave Harper Valley, he willingly accepted accountability for removing his family from the only home they had ever known, in a town they all held dear and cherished. Tyron and Megan seemed thrilled with the imminent flight that they were about to embark on, while Molly and Ryan stood inaudibly in a corner, holding onto one another, though knowing that in a short while, there would be far too much distance and detachment between them.

Molly glanced around her quickly and realized that Tyron and Megan were far too young and childlike to understand how diverse their lives would be. Tyron was two weeks away from turning thirteen, while Megan had just turned ten-years-old. She glanced at her father and realized that they had hardly spoken to one another in almost a week, yet, her rage and resentment towards him had remained unrelenting.

"Molly, I love you so much, always and forever." Ryan held Molly firmly against him, afraid that it may be the very last time they would see each other again. "Come back to me. I'll wait for you, and I will wait forever if I have to." He whispered desolately in her ear. Molly could scarcely breathe when it became clear to her that they were saying goodbye. She began gasping for air at the inevitability of leaving Ryan behind. She knew in her heart that tomorrow would be entirely divergent for them, and it terrified Molly to consider the very thought that Ryan could move on, without her. She was terrified that after a while, he might stop thinking about her, and when enough time had passed, he would inevitably, discover someone new to take her place. Molly's heart convinced her that she could under no circumstances leave him behind. Losing him was a probability that she was disinclined, and ill-equipped to envision.

"No!" She shouted out before she retreated from Ryan and ran towards James. "Daddy, please!" She grabbed his hands, undaunted by strangers that were witnessing her erratic behavior. "Daddy, I'm begging you!" She pleaded under extreme anxiety, while her tears found its way down her cheeks once more. Ryan approached James Starkey cautiously, "Mr. Starkey, please. Please let Molly stay, please?"

Maria turned to face at Sue, "Let her stay, we'll take good care of her?" She just about pleaded with Sue when she realized that Ryan and Molly could hardly live without one another. "Thank you, Maria, but she can't." James interrupted, before Sue could respond. He turned back to Molly, who was crying hysterically. "Molly, we talked about this?" "You, you did the talking, not me! You decided, not me!" She yelled out to him through her hysteria. "I don't want to go!"

James turned to Ryan, "I know that you feel affection for Molly, Ryan. Believe me, I wouldn't have it any other way, but if this association is meant to be; if you two are meant to be together at the end, she will come back to you, I promise." Ryan could hardly comprehend much of what her father was telling him, but he knew that he had to respect the decision James Starkey had made. It shattered Ryan's heart when he realized that nothing they could say, would alter the fact that Molly had to board that plane with her family and begin a new life in a new town, without him. He calmly led her back into the corner while unenthusiastically aware of the fact that there was nothing more any of them could do or say, to make Molly stay behind. He swabbed at the tears from his own eyes before lifting her head to face his. "Listen Molly, I'll wait for you. I promise. I will wait for you forever! Don't forget, don't ever forget how much I love you, and when times get bumpy, just think of me. Think of what we have. Think of what we've planned, and don't ever forget the promises we made to each other. We can do this, Molly, do you hear me? We can, you must believe it too." He kissed her delicately through her tears, while exasperatingly besieged to hold back his own. "I don't want to leave you." Molly cried out in desperation. "Molly, we can do this." He hastily whispered when he noticed James approaching them.

James took Molly's hand, and gently pulled her away from Ryan when the time had come to board the plane. "Ryan! Ryan!" Molly bellowed through her tears while under immense pressure to break free from her father, but Ryan turned and walked away from her when the tears began rushing down his own cheeks. Ryan could hardly stomach watching Molly leave his life. He could barely contemplate not seeing her each day, but primarily, he could not tolerate the veracity of what was taking place before his very eyes. For the first time in his life, he was powerless to come to Molly's aid when she needed him the most. Molly frantically fought to liberate herself from her father's grasp, but when she realized that he was not about to release her, she sunk into his arms, and sobbed violently once more while agonizingly alert to the anguished certainty that her heart was truly wrecked.

Molly

While ascending the stairway to the plane, Molly turned around one more time, and gazed at Joe and Maria one final time. She glanced around her and noticed Ryan standing at a distance behind them. She slowly lifted her hand to wave him goodbye. He waved back and smiled wretchedly, before he turned away from her for the last time. While driving back to Harper Valley with his parents, Ryan couldn't banish Molly from his mind. He was defenseless to dry the tears that were continuously rolling down his cheeks. Sorrow callously invaded his heart, and the confining lump in his throat seemed to grow larger. Ryan questioned whether they would be able to survive the separation and distance that had come between them. He became intensely afraid when he considered that Molly might soon meet new people. He was terrified that she would fail to remember him. It was a thought he could not tolerate. The only option left for Ryan was to maintain conviction in the life they had planned for, and faith that their love for one another would sustain them through the severance. He was convinced that the stars were performing malicious tricks on them equally, and that their perfect little world had come to an end. He prayed that their love would remain unchanged until the day they were united once again.

While gazing out of the window of the airplane, Molly felt sudden horror seize at her heart. She was desperately afraid that she might never see Ryan again or experience the way in which he so effortlessly loved her. Ryan constantly enforced feelings of shelter and warmth in her, yet, while she was seated on the plane, Molly all of a sudden felt apprehensive. She unexpectedly felt entirely alone when she constantly replayed him plead with her to return to him. Molly closed her eyes and thought back to the night they had made love for the first time. They had just returned home from a movie. As was the norm, Ryan suggested a walk on the beach with her before they made their way back home. They had taken extended walks before when they wanted to be alone, and they would quietly sit on the beach, contemplating their lives and strategizing for their future. That night was not unlike any other night, but it all changed when Ryan turned to her, and took her hands, "I'm going to marry you, one of these days, Molly." Molly could recall as though it was yesterday, how solemn he was at that moment. "I'm going to marry you too, Ryan." She let out a faint, but bashful giggle. There was nothing in the world that Molly desired more, than to spend the remainder of her life with Ryan Neves. He leaned in closer and gently kissed her. Molly realized once again how dearly she adored that schoolboy standing in front of her. His hands slowly made its way over her entire body, while Molly's body responded instinctively to his touch.

He made love to her that night on the beach, and told her

again and again, how desperately he adored her. For the first time in her life, Molly was certain that she had no life without him. She could in no way at all, consider an ordinary life without Ryan Neves. He was her first love, the only boy who could make her feel the way she felt. He was the only boy that Molly sought to give herself to without restraint. She had surrendered her heart to him a long time ago, but that night, he freely and unreservedly gave his heart to her.

As they got up from where they were lying on the beach, he placed his jacket around her when he discovered that she was trembling. "Are you okay?" He seized her in his arms and held her firmly against him. "I'm fine." She smiled at him, cognizant of the fact that her heart was hammering. For Ryan, making love to Molly for the first time was what surrendered her to him. There was no other girl in the entire universe that Ryan aimed to pursue, or to share the intimacy he had shared so enthusiastically with Molly. After that night, Ryan became increasingly shielding of her, and throughout their days at school, he ensured that they were together at all times, even attending the same classes as her. Ryan loved Molly more than he ever thought was possible. He would guard and preserve her with indescribable vigor. Ever since that night, Ryan was certain that he would give up his life to protect hers. He was reassured by the fact that Molly was absolutely and entirely devoted to him, and he could not predict a life without her. A life without them, without Ryan and Molly.

"Are you alright?" Molly heard her father's voice behind her. Even though she had remained incensed at him, the ache in heart was so much more powerful than Molly thought possible. Molly nodded without turning to face him. "I'll never be okay again." She thought sadly. They landed at the Rosewood International Airport almost two hours later when Molly was once again attentive to the restricting lump in her throat. She was distressed even more when she realized that it had engulfed her during the entire flight. "Come on, kids." She heard Sue scamper while handing each child their luggage. They had rented a car and drove for almost an hour before pulling up into an elongated driveway.

"This is our new home." James' broad smile was undeniable perceptible. Molly was at once irritated with her father's palpable pleasure, "We had a home, remember?" Molly could not control or suppress her anguish. When he parked the car in front of their new home, James instructed Sue to follow Tyron and Megan indoors. He turned to Molly, and clutched her hand, before leading her out into the unfamiliar garden.

"Molly, you are old enough to know and appreciate the circumstances surrounding our move. Perhaps I should've told you this sooner, but there was nothing much else I could do for us in Harper Valley. The industry was not doing well over there any longer, and relocating it inland was the only alternative I was left with. I have been able to secure two major contracts over here, and it ought to put the business back on the map." "You could've let me stay there, dad!" For an instant, James questioned whether he had made the right decision with Molly. "Molly, I love you. I can't leave you?" "Ryan loves me too, but I had to leave him! Dad, I love you, I honestly do, but I love Ryan too, and I have to be with him. He is who I am going to spend my life with, not you and mom! Not Tyron or Megan, but Ryan!" James placed his arms protectively around his daughter, "Someday, Molly, but until then, you are spending it with us. You can go and visit each holiday, my girl, I swear." James engaged in a feeble attempt to reassure his daughter while desperate to make himself feel a little less responsible for her broken heart.

Molly turned her back on him and made her way into the house that they would unenthusiastically call home from that moment on. Sue was waiting for Molly when she made her way indoors and led her daughter directly into her new bedroom. "We had someone move in the furniture," Sue casually began to engage with Molly, hoping to distract her. Molly wasn't paying attention, and impolitely interrupted her. "It doesn't matter, mommy." Molly flung herself onto her bed without hesitation or remorse. When she heard her bedroom door close behind her mother, she wept uncontrollably. Molly was fearful of what the future might hold for her. She was anxious that she would lose Ryan along the way, and desperately afraid of a life without him. She had no desire to seek out any new friends in their new town, even though her father was praying and furtively eager for her to meet new people and engage in new company.

Ryan was her only friend and to her, he was all that she had ever wanted. Molly swore to Ryan that she would write him a letter each week, and she looked forward to their future holidays together until the two remaining years were finally over. After graduation, there would be nothing that could keep them apart, and if she had worked assiduously at school, if she behaved in a manner that her father would approve of, there would be no basis for him to hold her back, and away from Ryan. For Molly, her life had begun with Ryan. She was by no means at all, prepared to allow James Starkey to eliminate him. For the time being, Molly had no authority over her life, and she was forced to linger until she had completed her final year at school.

Alice VL

HOME, FOR A WHILE

The last day of the first semester approached far too sluggishly for Molly. Ryan had written Molly a new letter each week, while Molly in turn responded almost without delay after reading his letters. Even though it was emotionally exhausting for both Ryan and Molly in the early days of her departure, Molly was able to only just endure the first semester without Ryan. He called her each night, and they would spend hours chatting to one another on the phone.

James would frequently stand at the door of his daughter's bedroom and eavesdrop, eager to listen in on their conversations. His daughter's feelings for Ryan were by no means tainted or distorted, and he secretly questioned why he and Sue never felt as profoundly connected with one another as Ryan and Molly felt with each other. He would occasionally nose around on her calls and hear her pledge to Ryan that she would return to him. It frightened James to consider that he couldn't compel her to remain without end, at home with her family. He predicted that the day would come that he would be forced to free her and let her go back to him, but for as long as he could, he was desperate to securely cling to her, and keep her close by.

At times, James would gaze at his daughter when she withdrew into a world that excluded him, and he couldn't help but wonder where his little girl had gone. He would query how disengaged he had become of her, and he tried to recall when they had last exchanged words with each other. He tried to reflect back to when she was only a little girl, but James knew that even then, she simply wanted to be around Ryan. He knew that if he forbade his daughter from contact with Ryan, or try and force her to make new friends, he would almost certainly lose her forever.

Before long, she would board a plane back to Harper Valley, and be reunited with Ryan once more for the holidays, after not quite three months had passed. Molly had gradually absolved her father for altering their lives so radically, and life at home more or less returned to normal. James repeatedly noticed how rigid it had been on Molly, and he realized in apprehension that she had no intention or longing to make any new friends. He mentioned to Sue that it troubled him enormously that she had so utterly sheltered herself from the outside world. She placed no magnitude on her classmates, and in no way ever, accepted any invitations to any social gatherings. If Molly was not chatting to Ryan on the phone, she was reclusively behind her desk writing him a letter. James grew progressively and extremely anxious of the intimacy in her affiliation with Ryan, but he once again reminded himself that it was too late to prevent any of it. Sue reminded him that Molly needed more time, but Molly no longer required any more time, she pined for Ryan.

James approached his daughter the night before with a plane ticket back to Harper Valley for a short visit with Ryan. "Come in!" Molly shouted when she heard a loud knock on her bedroom door. "Hello, Molly." James greeted her when he walked into her bedroom. "Hey, dad." She whispered hurriedly before she turned her attention back to her homework. "What are you doing?" He hesitantly sat down at the end of her bed. "Studying. Last exam of the term tomorrow!" "I have a surprise for you." He became excited in anticipation of witnessing his daughter's radiant smile once again. Molly took the envelope from him, and hurriedly opened it. When she discovered that it was her ticket back to Ryan, she leaped onto her father's lap, and held him steadily against her. "Thank you, daddy!" She kissed him on his cheek while unable to wipe the smirk off of her face. James forced a smile but was unexpectedly distressed to realize that he had virtually forgotten what Molly looked like when she was in high spirits.

He adored her smile and he frequently told Sue how her

Alice VL

smile could light up any hour of darkness he may find himself in. He was constantly aware of his daughter's flawless and childlike beauty, but when she smiled, he felt as though his world had become immobile. Considering how desperately despondent she had been over the past few months, he was almost certain that her spirit was crushed, and he regularly wondered what tactics fate had in store for them. It pleased him greatly to know that for once, he was responsible for a smile on her face, instead of being the constant source of her heartache.

Molly had only moments earlier turned in her final examination paper for the semester, when she swiftly and animatedly exited her classroom. As she grabbed her school bag, she breathlessly reached for her mobile phone, and dialed Ryan's number at once. "Molly?" "Ryan!" She hollered out in elation. "Mols, I miss you!" Molly interrupted him in next to no time. "Guess what?" She paused for a split second, "I'm flying out today!" Ryan sensed the immediate and inexorable exhilaration in her voice. "Are you coming back to stay?" Molly was at once sensitive to the extreme anxiety in his voice. "No, just for the holidays." "What time is your flight?" He was saddened that her visit would be only brief, but relieved that he could see her again, after what felt to him like forever. "I land at eight tonight!" "I'll be there. Oh, and Molly?" "Yes?" "I love you." Molly smiled, "I love you more!"

Alice VL

Molly

When Molly arrived home, Sue hurriedly helped her pack her luggage for her short holiday in Harper Valley. "Please be careful, honey." Sue gazed worriedly at her daughter while folding her jeans. "Oh, mommy! There's not much more in the world that I want, than to see Ryan." Molly took the pair of jeans from her mother and placed them in her suitcase. "Mommy, I know you and dad don't get it, but I wish so that you and dad can understand how much I love him. I need him so much in my life. It's as though I just can't get myself together without him." She was frantic for her mother to understand how desperately she needed to be with Ryan. Sue nodded dejectedly when she noticed the strain on Molly's face, at the same time, feeling unexpectedly ill-equipped when it came to finding the words that her daughter so desperately needed to hear, something to confirm to Molly that she understood, but as usual, the words failed her. She tried to recall when precisely it was that they had lost Molly, and with panic abruptly making its presence known to her, Sue accepted that it was from the moment she gave birth to her daughter. Molly in no way belonged to them, not even for a moment.

James and Sue drove Molly to the airport in silence. Molly smiled as she sat in the backseat of the car, imagining and dreaming of seeing Ryan again. James was miserable at the prospect of his daughter leaving for the holidays, but he reluctantly accepted that keeping her away from Harper Valley, may perhaps drive her further away from them. He could not disregard the warning that their connection was entirely disproportionate and excessively commanding at their youthful age. In the midst of all of these thoughts harassing his mind, James grudgingly accepted that what they felt for one another; was utterly extraordinary, and he could in no way dismiss it.

James had barely parked the car at the airport when Molly headed out directly to the departure counter. "Molly!" James called after his daughter before he engaged into a rapid trot, desperate to catch up with her. "Your flight is only in an hour. Wait for us!" Molly turned around to face her parents, but the pleasure on her face was impossible to overlook. James hooked his daughter's arm into his own, before they calmly walked up to the departure desk. Once James checked Molly in, Sue suggested that they enjoy a cup of coffee before Molly boarded her flight.

They had just placed their order when James turned to Molly, who was constantly glancing at her wristwatch. "Honey, we're going to miss you." "I'll miss you too, daddy." She caught a glimpse of her watch once again. "I've lost you a long time ago, haven't I?" Molly grimaced at once, "No dad, no. I love you. You're my daddy!" Molly was utterly distraught when she realized that her father was under the mistaken impression that she loved Ryan simply more than she did him. James was her conqueror, her superman of all heroes, while Ryan was her soul mate. "Daddy, I'm sorry, I don't mean to make you feel bad," She was frantic to enforce with him the fact that he was excessively significant and relevant to her, and her life. "My girl, don't be. I understand, or at least, I am trying to."

Molly was convinced that her father couldn't absorb her emotions, or could in any way comprehend her undying, devoted love for Ryan. Even as she gazed at her parents, Molly questioned whether they at all shared a diminutive speck of what she and Ryan had shared for an entire lifetime. When she turned back to face James, Molly flung her arms around his neck, "Daddy, I love you." For the first time in her life, Molly realized how unerringly and deeply, she worshipped her father. She smiled disconsolately at him, while Sue dabbed at a tear that had rolled down her cheek.

Molly climbed on the stairway that led her onto the plane. She turned back one more time to wave goodbye to her parents. "See you in a month! Love you guys!" She shouted out to them before she disappeared into the plane. Molly had only just settled in her seat when she thought of Ryan once again. She was abruptly aware of her tummy whirling, and the sudden feeling of anticipation that had crept up on her was slightly unsettling. For the first time in months, Molly felt truly animate and in high spirits again. She could barely wait to see Ryan again, she wanted nothing more than to feel his arms around her once more.

Alice VL

Molly

Molly began descending the flight of stairs after the plane had landed. She glanced around a few times before she finally caught sight of Ryan. "Ryan!" She yelled out before she began pushing through the crowds to unite with him. Ryan noticed her at once, and speedily made his way towards her. "Molly!" He seized her in his arms and turned her around and around. "Oh baby, I've missed you!" Ryan lifted her face and kissed her tenderly. "Ryan, I love you." "You've changed, you look different somehow?" Ryan whispered when he placed her back on her feet. "Have I?" Molly was uncomfortable almost at once. "I don't know what it is, but something is different about you? Come on, let's go!" He clutched her hand and led her to his car.

"I have a surprise for you." Ryan grinned mysteriously as they drove out of the airport. "A surprise? Tell me!" Molly tugged at his arm. "If I told you, it wouldn't be a surprise, would it?" Molly sat back and closed her eyes. She was immensely thankful that she could be with the man of her destiny yet again. "So, how is school?" "I hate it, Ryan. I hate everything about Park Hill!" "It's not the same here without you either, Molly."

After a short drive, they pulled up in front of the Garden Court Hotel in Murray Field. "What are we doing here, Ryan?" Molly questioned him in unexpected bewilderment. "I told you, it's a surprise." "Do your parents know?" "Yeah, sort of, but they said that they would deny they knew about any of this if your father ever found out" "Speaking of which, I just have to make a quick call to him, or else he'll be phoning all night long." The phone rang only once when she heard her father's familiar voice on the other side of the call, "Molly?" "Dad! Hi, I'm here! Safe and sound!" Molly explained hurriedly while attempting to hide the fact that he was the very last person she wanted to talk to at that very moment. "I trust that Ryan was there to meet you?" "Yes, of course, dad! Listen, I've got to go. My battery is dying and it's still a long drive to Harper Valley. I'll speak to you tomorrow. I love you and tell mom I miss her." Molly swiftly ended the call and without delay, she switched off her cell phone.

When they reached room 147, Ryan unlocked the door to the suite that he had reserved earlier. He smiled timidly at Molly as he tensely watched her. Molly was conscious of how unexpectedly inhibited she had become, and could in no way at all, identify with why she was reacting in such a subdued manner towards Ryan. Ryan nervously and carefully led her into the suite. She was astonished and flabbergasted by what was waiting for her. In the center of the bedroom, rested a large queen-sized bed covered in rose petals. She glanced past the bed when her eyes caught a bottle of sparkling wine that was placed on a dresser. Molly gazed over at Ryan, and unexpectedly became self-conscious once again.

Alice VL

Molly

"Molly, you know that I love you, right?" Ryan paused, before Molly nodded fearfully. He placed his arms around her and held her intimately against him. "Ryan?" "I have felt entirely alone and abandoned while you've been gone. I've missed you a great deal more than I thought was likely. For the first time in my life, I was without you, and it didn't get easier as time went on. I know that we're still far too young, but will you, will you marry me, someday? Will you *promise* to marry me?" Ryan held out a ring to her while pathetically aware that he had begun to quiver. Molly was unprepared for what he was asking her. It was incredible, but it was a question she could hardly have predicted quite so soon. She nervously gazed at Ryan and once more, she was entirely ambiguous about what precisely he was asking her.

"Molly, listen to me, we don't turn eighteen until early on next year. We can keep it quiet and continue with just being engaged until we graduate. Not a soul needs to know, until you get your high school diploma and am able to come back here." He rested his hands on her shoulders. "Ryan, yes, more than anything in the world, yes, but if I did something irresponsible now while I'm here, my dad would never let me see you again. Let's just, we just have to get through the next year and a half on my dad's terms. After that, there's nothing that can or will stop us. Except if you change your mind." "I love you, Molly, and I'll never change my mind." He began undressing her gradually, "You

Alice VL

are so beautiful." He kissed her fiercely, before he carried her to the large bed in the center of the bedroom. Molly's body began to respond to him once again. She was delighted and relieved that time had been unable to contaminate or distort a single fraction between them. It felt to her as though she had in no way at all, separated from Ryan. "Make love to me, Ryan."

"Molly, Molly, wake up." She indistinctly heard Ryan's comforting voice as she groggily attempted to open her eyes. When she spotted Ryan sitting next to her, she was ecstatic that she was not dreaming of his presence. "Molly, I want you to wear the ring around your neck. I want you to remind yourself each day of our pledge to each other, and that nothing can come between us, ever, okay?" He gently kissed her on the cheek. "I love you, Ryan." "We better get going, my parents are waiting for us." Ryan whispered before sliding on a pair of jeans and a t-shirt.

Alice VL

Molly

When they reached Harper Valley later that morning, Ryan and Molly headed directly for the Neves home. Molly was thrilled to be back in the town she treasured and longed for. She was pleased to see Joe and Maria again and felt like she had been gone for too long, but more than anything, Molly was elated when she realized that Ida and Louis were waiting there to meet them.

Ida was an incredibly close friend of Molly and Louis of Ryan. After years of eagerly hoping for a union between the two friends, Ida and Louis finally found their way into each other's hearts. Their unification was responsible for Ryan and Molly's palpable delight, they were absolutely thrilled that the two couples were the closest of friends.

Maria brought lemonade out to the pool, where the four friends discussed events and going-on's in Harper Valley. Although Molly was overjoyed absorbing all that was taking place in Harper Valley, she felt as though she was absent from her very own life. She no longer felt like a fraction of Harper Valley, while recognizing emotions of awful apprehension as she sat listening to their stories. Molly briefly discussed her life in Park Hill and admitted to absolutely loathing her new home. While there, she could barely pass the time in an attempt to come home, and she nonchalantly conceded to her friends that the concept of returning to the village that raised her, was all that she fixated on.

When Ida and Louis said goodbye later the afternoon, Molly was furtively relieved that they had finally left. She turned to face Ryan who took her firmly into his arms, frightened that time might make her forget how wonderful she felt when he took her into his arms. Molly closed her eyes and intimately recognized his scent.

After dinner, Ryan took Molly for an extensive stroll on the beach. "Molly?" Ryan turned to Molly before taking her hands. "Promise me that you will come back to me as soon as you can?" Molly sensed that he was almost beseeching her. "Ryan?" She was devastatingly insightful to the sudden mystification that had instantly invaded her heart. "It's just that, I feel, I feel that we are gradually shifting away from each other, and it scares me a little." Molly felt him tightening his grip on her hands. "Ryan, we *are* changing, we are growing up, and we can't stop that. We can't put a hold on who we will become, but we love each other. *That* can't change, that can never change, can it?" She was unexpectedly alert to trepidation engulf her entire being. "I will love you eternally, Molly, and I will dream of you every day of my life, and *that* will never change." He kissed her lovingly once again.

Alice VL

Molly

Each time Ryan kissed Molly, she knew into the core of her, that their devotion to one another would effortlessly sustain them through the next year and a half. "If anything ever goes wrong, just remember, you can come back to me, no matter what happens, no matter what you do, or what goes on around you, okay?"

For the remnants of the holiday, Molly and Ryan depleted each waking moment as one. Even though they regularly went around to Ida and Louis' place, they were utterly contented to be alone in isolation with only one other. Molly would often catch a glimpse of Ryan merely staring at her, and although she diligently hunted to absorb all there was about him, she discovered that it was as though she was seeing him, and all the pieces about him, for the very first time. She was dreadfully frightened that they might forget the little things about one another, and at the same time, it terrified her to consider that Ryan could drift away from her bit by bit, and plunge into a new love and a new association with someone else. It was a horror Molly could in no way discard or banish from her mind, and at times, the very contemplation became almost unbearable for her. At night, she would climb out of the bed she was sleeping in, and creep into Ryan's bedroom where they would fall asleep, holding one another intimately. Before sunrise, Ryan would wake her, and she would tiptoe back to her own bed before anyone noticed.

Molly was instructed to call her father every other day, and even though she missed her folks, she required nothing more than to subsist alongside Ryan. Joe and Maria tried yet again to sway James to allow Molly to return to Harper Valley, but as much as James empathized with his daughter's injured heart, he was adamant that she was far too immature to move such an enormous distance away from her parents. Above all, James was terrified of letting his daughter set out on a journey without him in it. He was convinced that he maintained a right to additional and valuable moments with her, and he was convinced that he had lost out on an enormous amount of time with Molly. James was by no means at all, equipped to surrender her to Ryan just yet, while Sue was abundantly aware of how daunting the circumstances surrounding Molly was impacting him.

The day before Molly was to return to Park Hill, she woke up beside Ryan, plagued by the tears which were shimmering in her eyes. "Ryan, wake up." Ryan opened his eyes slightly, "Molly?" Ryan rubbed his sluggish eyes while making a noble effort to focus on her. "Ryan, I don't want to go back." She distressingly buried her head into his chest. Ryan could at once sense that she was lamenting softly, yet he was powerless to alter James Starkey's decision. "Molly, let's get married. I don't want you to go home. I don't want you to leave again. Let's do it. Let's just do it." Molly could at once feel the hammering of her heart, her stomach turning, and a sickening feeling overwhelm her. "What?" She paused as she tried to gulp past the lump in her throat. "Ryan, my dad will never let us. He will never give us permission, let alone his blessing. I am not old enough to make that decision, legally." "Yes, I know we're not eighteen yet, but let's talk to our parents, let's *make* them to understand. What if you got pregnant? Let's run away. Let's go so far." Molly was devastatingly vulnerable to the tremendous anxiety in his voice, "No, Ryan, my dad will find us, and he will never let me see you again. He doesn't understand that my heart searches yours and will look for you until the day I die. He doesn't understand that I can't function, or even breathe without struggle, without you. He just doesn't understand, Ryan. Besides, it's only another year and a half, if I got pregnant now, he would never let met come back here. He'll never forgive me." She clasped his face in her hands when Ryan kissed her before he gazed amorously into her eyes. "Molly don't forget me. Hold on to this, to us. Don't forget us." Molly at once pulled herself together, rubbed her eyes, and smiled sadly, "You are home to me, Ryan. I wish I was braver."

Alice VL

Molly

GONE

When they reached the airport, Molly was deeply sensitive to an identifiable misery that had crept into her heart. It no longer mattered how often she would be mandated to leave Ryan; it would constantly torture and shatter her as profoundly as it did the very first time, she was forced to say goodbye to him. Parting with Ryan was almost as though she was leaving a fraction of her essence behind, and it chillingly reminded her of how utterly incomplete she was without him.

When the time had come for her to board the plane that would inevitably sweep her away from Ryan yet again, she turned back to him one more time, "Look at me, Ryan. I love you, please wait for me. Don't forget me. I am begging you, just don't forget me. I am so terrified, Ryan, that when I get on that plane, I will never see you again. I feel like, I just can't shake the feeling that something's wrong between us?" Ryan swallowed back on a lump that had just begun to overwhelmingly scare him. "Molly, you're scaring me. Don't say things like that. Remember just one thing, I love you. I love, *love* you." Molly wept violently into his chest, and when she gazed up at Ryan one last time, she was utterly convinced that his eyes had exposed his crushed heart.

When she climbed the stairway of the plane, she refrained from turning back to Ryan. Molly carried on walking up the stairway, again unable to detach herself from the nudging feeling that something was scarily off-beam between them. Molly felt that somehow, something had been distorted, and had inadvertently transformed without her taking notice. She couldn't help but feel that nothing would ever be the same again for them. When she closed her eyes, she felt abrupt horror make its way through her entire body, and she was certain that she would never see Ryan again.

James and Sue were delighted to welcome their daughter back home to them. "Welcome back, baby, did you enjoy your holiday?" James held his daughter firmly in his arms. "Yes, thanks dad." She tearfully responded while at the same time, James and Sue interrogated themselves as to how much more hurt and anguish their daughter could endure. Sue gazed intimately at Molly and noticed that there was an abnormal and unusual element regarding her daughter, only, she couldn't place her finger on what it was, nor could she fairly decide on what seemed so entirely disparate about Molly. "You all right, baby?"

Alice VL

Molly

"I'm fine, mom." Sue scuffled to dismiss the abrupt anxiety that had encompassed her. She was convinced that something was wide of the mark with Molly, and during the drive home from the airport, Sue wondered whether she should mention her trepidation to James. When she thought about how he could possible retort in response, she was determined to keep her qualms to herself for a while. Molly sat in the back of the car in silence while gently rubbing the ring around her neck, blissfully ignorant to her mother's unexpected and increased apprehension.

Alice VL

Molly

The fourth week of the new semester approached swiftly. It was on that first day that Molly awoke to feeling poorly. Her mother had served breakfast for the family, and although Molly regularly enjoyed breakfast with her brother and sister, she was overcome with queasiness that very morning. "Are you alright, lovey, you're as pale as a sheet?" Sue remarked anxiously when she noticed that Molly was incapable of ingesting her breakfast. "I'm, I'm not feeling so good, mom?" "I can see that. Get back into bed. I'll call Dr. Neethling for a consultation." Sue at once reached for the telephone directory. "Molly?" James ran into her when he passed her in the hallway. "It's okay, dad, probably just something I ate." She had barely reached the restroom when she felt all inside of her push up. Sue found her in the bathroom, and hurriedly wiped her face down with a damp cloth. "Honey, is there something I should know?" Molly frowned at her mother, "Like what, mom?" "I don't know, perhaps why you might be feeling like this?" "I don't know what's wrong with me, mom!" Molly became agitated without forewarning. "Okay then, your appointment is in an hour. Have a bath before we leave."

When Sue shut the bathroom door behind her, she abruptly recognized why she had considered her daughter's dissimilarity before. She felt inexorable anxiety creep into her heart, and at that instant, while Sue Starkey stood on the other

Alice VL

side of the bathroom door, she was convinced that their daughter would never be the same after that day. Molly was finally lost to them for evermore.

"Molly Starkey?" A nurse at the doctor's consultancy called out, while signaling for Molly to follow her. "Come through, please." She hurriedly led her into Dr. Neethling's office. "Would you like me to come with you?" Sue asked just before Molly vanished around the corner. "No, I'll be fine, thank you, mom." Molly followed the nurse narrowly, and after taking a quick sample of her urine, and swiftly examining her blood pressure, Dr. Neethling showed her to a seat directly across from him.

"Molly, how old are you?" "I'm seventeen?" She whispered and began to tremble unexpectedly. "Do you have a boyfriend, Molly?" "Yes, I do, why?" Molly frowned, utterly puzzled by the perplexity of his questions. "Are, are you sexually active?" Molly's heart began thrashing at the rate of freight train. "Dr. Neethling, why are you asking me all these bizarre questions? What's wrong with me?" "Frankly, I don't know how to tell you this. You're pregnant, you're going to have a baby." Molly was appalled as she listened to what Dr. Neethling was casually informing her of. Her heart began to batter at a velocity she would imagine a jet plane to be going. She could barely take in air and was at once aware of the repulsion of her condition.

"Molly? Are you alright?" Dr. Neethling made his way to where she was seated, anxious that she might faint. "What are, what are you saying, doc?" Molly was convinced that he was teasing, but when he remained silent; when there was no suggestion at all that he had engaged in banter with her, Molly felt the blood drain from her face instantly. "It can't be. I am on the pill. I have been on contraception for months. How?" Molly was utterly baffled and unprepared for the verdict. "Molly, birth control pills are only 99% effective. Have you taken any other medication recently?" "I, don't, yes, I was taking antibiotics for a sinus infection a month or so ago?" "Well, there you have it then, antibiotics work against the pill."

He made his way back around to his desk. Molly stared at him in utter horror and entire disbelief. She could once again sense a restricting lump in her throat, not only threatening to open a floodgate of tears, but promising to restrict air to her lungs. "What am I going to tell my parents?" Molly was certain and without doubt that her father would never pardon her for disappointing him in such a sub-standard way. She was copiously conscious of the fact that all he had asked of her, was to graduate from high school before returning to Ryan. Her body began to shudder ferociously as she contemplated James' repulsive response. It terrified her to consider precisely how he might react.

"Would you like me to talk to them?" Dr. Neethling approached her sympathetically when he discovered that Molly had begun to quaver. Molly deliberated about it for a moment but concluded that no matter who it was that informed her parents of her current and sordid condition, there was nothing she could do to conceal if from them. She nodded nervously before Dr. Neethling buzzed the front office nurse. "Cindy, please ask Mrs. Starkey to come through."

Sue abruptly entered his consulting room where she discovered her daughter in severe distress. "What's the matter, baby?" She anxiously placed her hands on her daughter's shoulders. "Mrs. Starkey, please have a seat." Dr. Neethling showed her to an empty seat beside her daughter's. "Molly, Molly says that she was taking antibiotics a while back, is this accurate?" "Yes, she had a minor sinus infection, why do you ask?" Sue intriguingly turned back to face her daughter. "Mrs. Starkey, antibiotics and birth control pill contradict one another, and …" Sue interrupted while glaring directly at Molly. "You're pregnant?" Molly could sense shock and annoyance in her mother's trembling voice. She began to whimper at once, unable to look her mother directly in the eye, but certain that she detected revulsion in her eyes just moments before. "I'm sorry, mommy." Sue was forlorn when she took Molly's hands into hers. "We'll work something out, it's all right. It's just your father, this is going to break his heart." Molly knew once again that her father would never exonerate her for what she had unintentionally done.

When they climbed into the car, Sue turned to her daughter. "You should tell Ryan." Molly nodded her head and began to snivel yet again. She was terrified of how her father would react to the uninvited sequence of events, but she found instant comfort in the belief that Ryan would be more compliant and tolerant of the quandary she found herself in. They drove the rest of the way in total silence, and when they reached their home, Molly was thankful that her father had left for work. "I'm going to call your father." Sue took her mobile phone from her purse. "Mommy?" Molly tried to find some form of reassurance from her mother. "We must deal with this now, Molly. There's no point in putting it off. The sooner, the better."

"James, could you come home, please?" Molly couldn't hear what her father's response was, but she engaged in a courageous effort to remain focused on her mother's voice. "No, nothing, just come home, James." Sue abruptly ended the call and took an empty seat at the dining room table while incessantly fidgeting with her phone. When James arrived home, almost fifteen minutes later, Sue and Molly were seated in silence at the dining room table, restlessly and impatiently awaiting his presence. "What's wrong, baby?" James asked nervously just as he noticed tears in both Sue and Molly's eyes. He turned to face Sue, "Sue?" Molly knew her father well, and the tone in his voice confirmed to her that he was growing apprehensive. "She's pregnant, James." Sue bowed her head, desperate to avoid the fury she knew was about to show up on James' face.

James stared at Sue, overcome by incredulity, before he turned to face Molly. "Molly?" She was instantly responsive to the shock and disbelief in her father's voice. "I'm sorry, daddy." Molly was about to explain when James exasperatingly interrupted her.

"Sorry? Is that all you can say?" Molly had erupted into desolated tears, and she could barely respond to her father. "This is what I get? This is the thanks I get for sending you on a holiday to him. This is how you earn my trust, Molly? I suppose now you're going to tell me you and Ryan want to get married?" He continued to roar at her while pacing up and down. Molly had no allusion of what to say to him, and even though she could come up with a brilliant defense, there was nothing she could say to alter his outlook on her unexpected condition. "I didn't do this on purpose, daddy!" "I can't believe anything you say anymore, Molly. Give me your mobile phone!" Molly lifted her phone and handed it to her father. "Does Ryan know?" Molly shook her head, and when he turned to Sue, she confirmed it by shaking hers. "As from this day forward, you are grounded! No mobile phone, and no contact with Ryan! Do you understand me! Not today, not tomorrow, not ever again!" He paused for a brief moment, "You are never to see that boy again, Molly, never!" "Daddy, please, no!" Molly got up from her seat, and frantically tried to take James' hands into hers, but he repelled her almost at once. "Mommy!" Molly urgently yelled out for her mother to step in, but Sue remained silent. Sue resigned herself to the fact that in the innermost part of her, there was nothing she could do for Molly. "James?" Was all Sue could say while fixating her eyes on him, hoping that she shouldn't have to say much at all. By the expression on Sue's face, he at once detected that she by no means saw eye to eye with him, and he was positive that he could perceive traces of pure repugnance for him in her eyes.

"I want to speak to Ryan!" Molly bellowed out, overcome by tremendous anxiety, her voice shuddering irrepressibly, and desperate to convince her mother to allow her to make that call to Ryan. James had since walked out, but instantly rushed back in, "you'll tell Ryan nothing! You know that you can't keep the baby! It will ruin your life! What do you think it will do to Ryan's?"

Molly

He became overwhelmingly infuriated once more. "You're seventeen, Molly, you're still a baby yourself!" Molly could no longer bear to listen to him heartlessly roar at her, "You are ruining my life, dad!" "What life, Molly? What is there to ruin? No, you cannot have this baby. The only thing to do is to, to get rid, to have a, to terminate the pregnancy." He staggered over his words as he was unexpectedly aghast while listening to himself verbalize what was going on in his mind. "Dad! You can't even say it, but you are asking me to kill a life inside of me?" James lowered his head at once, "I am not asking you. It's not a request. You *will* take care of it. None of this is negotiable, Molly."

Sue was totally taken aback by what he had ordered. She glared at him overcome with rage and apprehension, unable to accept as true that the man that she had been married to for so many years, was capable of an act as horrendous as such. "James?" Sue leaped from her chair and faced him directly in the eye, "Listen to me, Sue, Molly cannot keep the baby. She's seventeen years old! No, she must have an abortion. It's the only way that Molly can regain control of her life, and eventually make something of what's left of it." "James, there are alternatives. We, as her parents can step up, and help her raise the baby. That's our job, James. She made a mistake. We are there to guide her through her mistakes, James. That's what parents do. And, if you truly have no interest in being a supportive father, what about adoption? How could you even ask her to have an abortion?" Sue engaged in a heroic combat with her husband in a frantic attempt to reason with him, while wholly stunned and shaken by what he was suggesting. "I am not asking, Sue! You misunderstand! Adoption only means she will *still* be carrying the baby, what don't you understand? She will neglect her classes and her obligations to her schoolwork! No, she cannot have this baby! Raising her child will still expose her to motherhood, Sue!"

James was extremely strong-willed, and his mind was instantly made up. Molly could no longer tolerate any more of the grueling arguments. She abruptly ran upstairs to her bedroom where she threw herself onto her bed. "Ryan." There was no way at all that she could reach out to him, and even though she was somehow able to get in touch with him, her father would never allow her to return to Ryan.

James found her in her bedroom later that evening. Molly was reminded once again of his utter anger and extreme disappointment. "Here." He involuntarily handed her back her mobile phone. "I want you to call Ryan, and tell him that it's over, that you won't see him again, and more importantly, that you don't *want* to see him again." Molly sat straight up on her bed, and could once again, barely consider what her father was compelling her to do. By the expression on his face, she was certain that no matter how desperately she begged and pleaded with him, he would on no account ever, giver her permission to tell Ryan of their child. "Daddy?" She began to sob feverishly. "Please don't do this, daddy." James turned away from her, inflexible and unyielding in submitting to his daughter, yet convinced that he was acting in her best interests. "Molly, if you ever, ever want an opportunity at a normal life again, you'll make the call." He responded harshly. "I *have* a normal life, dad, with Ryan. I love him, daddy." Molly was desperately anxious for her father to understand and appreciate that she was still Molly, the daughter he highly thought of and vastly regarded for seventeen years. "You love him? You are under my roof, and as long as you are here, you will do exactly as I say, or so help me, I will send you far away, Molly, and you'll never, ever see any of us again!" The anger in his heart had escalated at a rapid speed. Molly felt bullied but was certain that he had every intention of making good on his threats. "Then let me go, daddy, let me go to Ryan!" "Make that call Molly!"

While cautiously dialing Ryan's number, Molly felt coerced into making a call that she never thought she would be compelled to make. She was certain that a fraction of her was dying inside, and she prayed feverishly that Ryan would miss her call, but when she heard his voice, she knew that there was no turning back. James was standing silently, yet firmly beside her and glaring wrathfully at her. She finally accepted that she was forced to comply with her father's ruling, even though he was harrying her into doing something she had no voice or opinion in. He had appointed himself her judge, her jury, and more painfully, her executioner.

"Molly?" "Hey …" She bravely attempted not to choke on her words. "You okay, baby?" When he sensed her despair, he knew once again that something was highly out of place with Molly, and he instinctively felt that the call would alter the path they had taken. "No, I, Ryan, I just called to ask, to tell you not to contact me again." She surrendered and gave up on trying to hold back her tears as she sobbed violently into the phone. James stood glaring at his daughter, unwavering that Molly was obliged to end her relationship with Ryan. He knew that he was drumming the final nail into her heart, but he was convinced that there was no other solution. Ryan was overcome with trepidation as he tried to force her to clarify what had happened, but she cut him off almost at once. "I don't want to see you again, Ryan, never, it's over. Just forget me. Forget everything, it was stupid, just forget."

Molly hung up exasperatedly, frightened that if she had stayed on the line with him for only a moment longer, she would blurt all out to Ryan. She couldn't risk him discovering the truth about the baby. Molly was certain that her father would ruthlessly penalize her and keep her locked away from Ryan forever.

"Molly! Molly!" Ryan hollered into the phone, desperate for her to respond, anxiously hoping to hear her voice, but convinced that there was no-one on the other side of the call. As if in a wandering haze, Ryan slowly placed the phone down beside him. He was confused and failed to comprehend why Molly had so abruptly and unexpectedly discarded him. He immediately called on Ida, and vigorously questioned her about Molly, but Ida had no penchant as to what was taking place between them. As with Ryan, Ida was absolutely staggered, but she promised to call him the moment she had established contact with Molly.

Ryan called Molly's mobile phone once more but was at once disillusioned when he reached her voice mail. James snatched the phone from Molly immediately after she had ended her call to Ryan, and swiftly removed the battery. As he was about to exit her bedroom, he turned back one last time, "It's for the best, Molly, you'll thank me for this one day." He made a desperate attempt to convince himself that he was doing what was best for Molly, even though he had a nudging feeling that it may be the biggest mistake he would ever make with her. He knew deep down that Ryan was what was best for Molly, but he shrugged off that little voice inside that was letting let him know in no uncertain terms, that he was crushing her spirit. "I will never thank you for this, you destroyed my heart! I will never, *ever* forgive you for this!" She shouted out in extreme anxiety when he walked out of her bedroom.

He had just placed mobile cell phone in the safe in his bedroom when he heard his own phone ring. "Starkey?" "Hi, Mr. Starkey, it's Ryan." James cut him off without hesitation, "Ryan, don't call us again, and don't try and contact Molly. She's met someone else, and it's for the best that you accept it." Ryan felt his heart blow up into a thousand pieces when he listened to what James Starkey was telling him. His heart reminded him that Molly would never betray him, or turn her back on him, and he unexpectedly felt constrained by a well-known restriction in his throat. "I, I don't believe you, sir." "It's true, Ryan. Didn't she just tell you to never contact her again? Goodbye, son." James abruptly ended the call, while copiously aware of the fact that he was the one person betraying both Ryan and Molly.

James sat at the end of his bed and felt a colossal amount of guilt for what he had done only moments before, yet he consoled himself believing that it was his love for Molly that drove him to cling to her for just a while longer. James had exceptionally elevated hopes and even larger dreams for his daughter, and he was in no doubt that if she had held onto her baby, it would all be taken away from her, and be lost to her forever. Molly deserved an opportunity to aspire for the stars, and he frantically wanted her to reach out, and grab a hold of all the accomplishments he was certain she could effortlessly attain.

He listened to Molly sniveling in her bedroom, and was reminded of his own agonizing sting, but he was positive that Molly would recover from this juncture in her life and move on fluently when enough time had passed. He convinced himself that he was acting as a good father, even though he knew that Molly would never move beyond his bullying her into lying to the boy she had loved for her entire life. For just a moment, James hesitated before he finally acknowledged that they were doing what was right for all concerned.

Ryan was utterly overwhelmed and distraught when James informed him of the fact that Molly had found a new love, and it ripped at his very core. He sat outside until the stars came out, trying to comprehend how it was possible that Molly could disregard him as effortlessly as she did. It made no sense to him whatsoever, and he could hardly shake the feeling that she had perhaps, never loved him at all. He switched off his mobile phone, and vowed never to speak with reference to her, or to make contact with her ever again. Ryan was determined to change his phone number the very next morning and move on with his life, without Molly, just as she desperately yearned for. He was determined to erase all traces of Molly from his life, as though she never existed.

Alice VL

Molly

Sue clutched at Molly's hand when they entered the St. Anne's clinic on a cold and windy morning not long after Molly had broken up with Ryan. She had scheduled the appointment for Molly a week before, after discovering an advertisement in the local newspaper. Even though it was a solution that she by no means believed in, and in no way sought to be a fraction of, Sue was swayed that James would never, modify his train of thought, or mull over an alternative solution. Sue by no means did much of anything that was in opposition to James' will, but she felt in her heart, that he had made an immoral verdict, and she prayed for him to alter his decision at some point, before it was too late.

She tried discussing Molly's state of affairs with James the night before, but he had no inkling or desire to discuss it any further. He irately insisted that Molly would stand no chance at a reputable life with a baby, and he was convinced that she and Ryan were not ready for the responsibilities that came with raising a child. When she finally realized that James had reached a steadfast decision, Sue resigned herself to the fact that an abortion would be the only decision James would ever make at this point in Molly's life. Molly tried to call Ryan after their last exchange of words when she snuck her mother's phone out of her purse, but he refused taking her calls. She was certain that he was avoiding her after the harsh and brutal way she spoke to him. More than anything, she was distressed by her father's detachment from her, and she was once again reminded of the fact that she had disappointed him far beyond her wildest imagination.

"Mommy, please, don't make me do this. Please let me talk to Ryan, please mommy, I am begging you." Molly pleaded with her mother to allow her to make one final call to Ryan, but Sue pretended not to hear. After taking their seats in the waiting area, Molly was doubtful that there was anything she could do or say, to compel her parents to identify with, and accept the love she had for Ryan. There was nothing she could say to persuade them to allow her to keep her baby. She wanted to tell them that they could work it out, and that somehow, they would cope with the baby together, but more than that, she wanted to implore them to give her an opportunity to prove to them that they could trust her. She acutely sought after her parents to accept and understand that Ryan would never turn his back on her. Molly, to a great extent, was keen to let them see the ring Ryan had given her and tell them about the vow they had once made to one other. Of all the things she longed to tell them, she yearned for them to realize how overwhelmingly she cherished Ryan, but while her mind was racing around in circles, Molly unwillingly accepted that her father had no interest or willingness to pay attention to her.

Molly

"Ms. Starkey?" She heard a nurse call out for her. "Go on." Sue compassionately wiped the tears that had begun to roll down her daughter's cheeks, while utterly sensitive to the tears in her own eyes. Molly reluctantly got up from her seat, and for a brief moment, she considered running from them. She wondered if she would be capable of placing distance between her and her parents, while frantically finding her way back to Ryan. Molly knew that no matter how fast she ran from them, they would find her, and bring her back. All that was left for her to do was to move onward, and slaughter her and Ryan's child. She couldn't help but reflect on the following day, when her father would act as though none of it had ever take place. He would go about his day-to-day routine, as though it had never happened. Molly knew that Ryan would in no way ever absolve her for all she had inflicted on him in only a matter of days. She saw no point in fighting her parents any longer. Just as severe as James' betrayal was for her, so was her treachery towards Ryan. Molly was confident that Ryan would have stood by her had she had given him the option.

She called Ida on two occasions after her phone call to Ryan, beseeching her to convince Ryan into taking her call, but Ida was defenseless to sway him. Ida repeatedly questioned her on what exactly had taken place between them, but Molly was mortified by her situation, and devastatingly ashamed of what she was about to do. Ida made a valiant effort to pressure Ryan into listening to what Molly had to say, but he resolved to never speak to her, or see her again, convinced and overwhelmed by the fact that she had chosen someone else.

The surgical ward into which the young nurse showed her into was gloomy and chilly. Molly was deathly terrified, and felt her world entirely disintegrate around her. She hesitantly changed into a hospital robe, and almost as though in a wander haze, she climbed onto the bed when she noticed the surgeon approaching her. "Are you alright?" Molly failed to pay attention to him. All she could think of was Ryan, and how she was betraying not only him, but herself too. "Help me, Ryan." Molly whispered silently, sensitive to the devastating reality that Ryan wasn't coming to rescue her. Overcome by wretchedness, Molly was so sure that he had effortlessly forgotten, and discarded her. She turned her thoughts to her father, and while he had refused to speak to her since he discovered her pregnancy, she convinced herself that she would be forced to make a mammoth effort to salvage his confidence in her once again.

While she lay staring at the ceiling of the surgical ward, Molly was no longer troubled by the fact that he no longer had faith in her. She lost reliance in him the moment he abandoned her and her beliefs, the day that he ordered her to undergo an abortion, and the instant he pressured her into saying a final farewell to the one single person that gave her life meaning. Molly's heart was shattered, and while lying there, waiting to end the life of their child, she knew that she would never recover from her loss. Molly never once expected to be disappointed by her father, until that day; the day she was in for a rude awakening.

Alice VL

Molly

When Molly opened her eyes, her mother was firmly stationed beside her. "Are you in much pain, lovey?" She bent down to kiss her on her forehead. "I hate you, I hate dad, but more than that, I hate you." Molly muttered irately as her tears rolled steadily down her cheeks. Sue could barely detect what it was that she was mumbling, but positive that she was dazed from the effects of the general anesthetic. She helped Molly get dressed, and in silence, walked her out to their car. Molly was completely under the manipulation of the anesthetic and could think of nothing else other than returning to sleep. "Come on." Sue helped her daughter climb into the car. They drove home in silence, and regardless of the fact that Sue was perceptive to the grief that her daughter was introduced to, she prayed that perhaps James would vindicate his daughter, and get back to the way things were between them. Her heart reminded her that they could never carry on as they had before, and she knew into the very core of her that Molly never deserved her father's wrath.

When she glanced over at Molly, Sue was in no doubt that their striking daughter was tainted, and that they single-handedly were accountable for the obscurity that had entered her life as an unwelcome guest. The sorrow and disillusionment in her daughter's eyes was an apparition that Sue never wanted to witness even once, and she found it despicable that they, as her parents, had inflicted utter destruction onto their daughter.

Alice VL

Molly

Sue placed her hand on Molly's shoulder, but Molly cringed at her mother's touch despite the fact that she gazed directly ahead of her, refusing to surrender to her mother's compassion. Sue was at once alert to a smoldering sensation into the core of her when she realized that Molly should never have experienced such immense murkiness, as she had that very day. She was painful aware hat she did not guard or defend her daughter, and she knew that the Molly they had adored and cherished, had vanished forever.

Once they arrived home, Tyron and Megan were playing with James on the front lawn. When he heard the car pull into the driveway, James turned to glance at Molly for just a moment, but quickly turned his focus and attention back to Tyron and Megan. "I'm going to bed." Molly was instantly reactive to the observable repugnance in her father's eyes. It instantly allowed her tears to gush unreservedly. Molly refused dinner that evening. It was only when Sue had brought her a glass of balmy milk that Molly accepted that it was all over. "Give your dad some time, Molly." Sue was desperately trying to save the link between a father and daughter that she was covetous of so many times before. "Give him time, you say?" Molly paused to take a sip of her milk, "Why should I give *him* time? I don't *care* what he thinks of me! I don't care how he feels! I don't care! I hate him, mom, *and* I hate you! You should've stopped him! You could've stopped him! Why didn't you? Why? You are my *mother*, and that's what mothers do! You and dad taught me that taking another life is wrong! You, mother, how many times haven't I heard you oppose the fact that abortion is legal in our world? How many times didn't you say that it should be abolished in the name of God? You and dad are both liars and hypocrites, and I will never believe anything you say, ever again!"

Molly was right, and it was with those words that Sue realized once again that they had inadvertently severed all ties to their daughter. There was not a soul else to blame, but themselves. They couldn't hold Ryan accountable for any of their chaos. From the moment that Molly had discussed the intimacy of their relationship with Sue, she simply recommended that Molly familiarize herself with birth control methods. They did very little to try and bring to an end, the relationship between Ryan and Molly. The sequence of ill-fated events that unfolded of late, they alone were liable for.

When Sue made her way downstairs, she stumbled upon James in the passageway, "How is she?" Sue was at once aware of the overwhelming concern in his voice. She was certain that she should never have allowed James to force their daughter to go against her own wishes. "You, may God forgive you, because I, I can't. Everything we ever taught our children were lies! She will never forgive us, James, but more than that, I will never forgive myself for not putting my foot down. This was a mistake!" Sue whispered hoarsely before she turned away from him.

When James checked in on Molly later on in the evening, he felt his heart shatter into a thousand pieces, watching her sleep. James was instantaneously aware of the painful truth that Molly would be unable and unwilling to excuse him for what he enforced upon her. While his heart was being ripped out from inside of him, he doubted whether he would ever be equipped to absolve himself. He reflected back to when she was just a little girl, and even though she had always adored Ryan, it was him that she turned to when she was wounded, or when she needed him. Molly had conviction in her father, but he betrayed his daughter, and he unexpectedly wished that he could reverse time to just a few hours back, so that he could assemble himself and re-assess her situation. She was his daughter, and he owed her a great deal more than what he presented her with. He silently wondered whether it would have been so dreadful for her to keep the baby, and he questioned all he thought he knew about Ryan and Molly. For a moment, he was certain that they were ready and equipped to find a solution, and make it work. His mind nudged him of the fact that they would have been alright, but more importantly, that their job with Molly would never be done, and helping her raise her baby was all part of raising Molly. Still, at the same time, his heart reprimanded him, and implored him to hold onto her for just a minute longer.

When he climbed into bed, he turned to Sue, and placed his arms around her. She was far too exasperated to respond and pretended to be asleep. "I'm sorry, Sue. I should've listened to her. How, how do I fix this?" Sue knew without reservation that it was too late. There was nothing in the world they could do to take Molly back to yesterday, and protect her heart, and her baby. When James realized that she wasn't reacting to him, he turned onto his back and lay staring at the ceiling, all the while envisioning the agonizing tears in Molly's eyes. It was an image he couldn't eject from his mind, and it performed like a play repeatedly, until he finally drifted off to sleep.

Alice VL

THE WAY HOME

"Are you ready for your big day?" The day that Molly had been waiting for, for the past eighteen months, had finally arrived. It was the day that Molly would graduate from high school, which would finally hand her the independence she had been craving ever since James had turned his back on her. It was a moment she was counting on, to depart from her parents. For months preceding her graduation, Molly planned her leaving home in the finest of details, and she could barely contain her enthusiasm to set out on her journey to find Ryan again.

Molly had not once since their last phone call, the day her father mandated her to call Ryan and break his heart, heard from, or spoken to him, and even though Ryan once swore to her that he would never let her go. Despite his promises, she was positive that that was unerringly what he did. When Molly secretly tried to call him in the months after, she was devastated when she found that his number was no longer in use. Ida not at all mentioned Ryan to her, and Molly was convinced that he had moved on without her. She was overwhelmed by all the thoughts running around in her mind, while lingering in bewilderment, and persuaded that Ryan's love for her had elapsed. She depleted her nights yearning for him, and when she closed her eyes, she couldn't get the vision of him standing at the airport, saying goodbye to her, out of her mind. She remained in her bedroom when she arrived home from school, and scarcely uttered a word to her father, given that he presented her with no alternative in the slaying of her unborn child. She worked inexorably hard at school to guarantee that she would not spend a moment longer at home than she should have to. When Molly was to finally receive her high school diploma, there would be nothing at all that her father could do, to keep her tucked away in Park Hill any longer.

"I've been ready for the last eighteen months. I can't wait to get out of here." Sue was at once saddened by Molly's harsh and frosty tone. "Molly, you don't mean that?" "Oh, but I do mom, and if I never see you or dad again, it will still not be long enough." She abruptly became silent before she picked up her luggage and walked out of her bedroom.

When Molly turned eighteen earlier on in the year, she was given access to a diminutive trust fund her grandparents had traditionally established for her when she was no more than a little girl. Molly bought herself a small, inexpensive used car, and a modest townhouse in Murray Field of which her parents had no knowledge of as she was preparing and designing her life in detail. She loaded her luggage into her car and headed out to school while devotedly attentive of the fact that her parents were trailing behind her. Molly was parting from them eternally. All she could think of when she glanced at her parents, was how they heartlessly destroyed her life and future with Ryan. She was unresponsive on the inside when she was around James and Sue, and she once again realized that it was a sentiment she had become too vividly acquainted with. After the unenthusiastic abortion, James simply did not have the audacity to thrash out what had taken place between them, it was far too tardy to try and set things right with Molly and Sue.

He avoided Molly at all costs, whereas the culpability he grudgingly took liability for, was by no means, ready to let him go any time soon. There were moments that he was anxious to take his daughter into his arms and let her know how hauntingly remorseful he was for what he had done, but he could hardly bring himself to confess his regret to Molly. He repeatedly deliberated on Ryan, and wondered whether he was waiting for Molly as he once swore he would. James knew without reservation that he had wrecked a love story he would so often be in awe of. He destroyed all that was important and valuable to his daughter, and in the process, he shattered a little fraction of himself and Sue. He vowed that he would never put Tyron or Megan through an ordeal as such, and he wished that he had simply known better with Molly.

Ryan had graduated from high school the year before Molly did. He accepted a proletarian job in England while he remained unrelenting with his studies. He was desperate to be gone from all the familiar faces, and all the well-known places that constantly reminded him of Molly. Months prior to his leaving, he had written Molly a letter to tell her of his leaving, but as was always the case, his mail was returned to him unreciprocated. It was at that instant that he disconsolately accepted that all that had taken place between them, was a painful reality, one he hadn't been able to admit to before. The girl he had loved and cherished for the largest part of his life, was eternally gone from him. Ryan unintentionally evolved into one of those men he found insufferable, the sort that would romance a beautiful young girl with the one and only purpose of bedding her, lacking any intention of ever seeing her again. The second he became too familiar around another woman, he would completely withdraw, and steer clear of her at all costs.

Louis was persistently alarmed by his friend's erratic and ungentlemanly behavior, and frequently tried to discuss Molly with him. Ryan would become enraged during any attempt to converse about Molly, leaving Louis to shun the issue entirely. What Louis was ignorant of was that Ryan never stopped thinking about Molly, and the life she was once a part of. Once in a while when the world was asleep, he would fish out a photo album he kept veiled in his closet and reminisce about their life as one. Ryan would hanker after her, but he never had the valor to face her again. He would lie at night with memories of her, and when he closed his eyes, it was only Molly he could see. He habitually thought about her, while frantic to memorize the little details about her. Ida would constantly become aware of how isolated he was becoming, and she knew in her heart that it was Molly he was obsessing about.

After the graduation ceremony, Molly hurriedly made her way back to her car. She was unprepared to find James waiting for her, and it tremendously disconcerted her to notice him standing there. "Molly …" She could hear his trembling voice and noticed that his hands were shuddering. Molly stood motionlessly in front of him, and for the first time in months, she interrupted her father without allowing him an opportunity to say what he evidently needed to tell her. "You know, dad, I still love Ryan, maybe even more than I used to. You forced me to do something that I would never have normally done, something I didn't believe in, but most of all, something that you taught me was *wrong*. You made me question everything I believed in, and you made me reassess everything you ever taught me. You made me butcher my baby without giving me an option to try and figure it out, to work it out with Ryan. I *know* that I made a mistake, and I know that I let you down, but you made me pay for it in the worst way imaginable. You murdered me that day too, dad, but the most awful thing that you ever did, was to make me say goodbye to Ryan, and I will hate you for that every day of my life. I will spend the rest of my life running away from you. I will place distance between us, and I will dedicate my life to never, *ever* forgetting what you did to me. You turned your back on me when I needed you the most and for that, I will in no way ever pardon you. I will never come back here, so don't ever try and find me. There is nothing you can do to stop me from leaving." She blurted out in one single breathe all that she had considered necessary, and all that was overdue.

James tried to take her hand, but she pulled free, anxious to get away from him, from the man who had ruined her life. As Molly drove off, she glanced in her rear-view mirror, and was taken aback when she saw him standing there unresponsively, certain that she saw him wiping tears from his eyes. Molly felt no kindness towards him. She wanted him to suffer pain, just as he forcefully familiarized her with destruction. She hoped that he still prized her as his daughter, just so that she could disappoint him again and again. She prayed that he experienced the same vulnerability and defenselessness that had come into her life not too long ago.

Alice VL

Molly

NOTHING IS THE SAME ANYMORE

Molly arrived at her townhouse in Murray Field shortly after ten that same night. It was a long and drawn-out drive for her, but she was in high spirits and overjoyed by the mere suggestion that there was a great deal of distance between her and her folks. Molly became gloomy when she thought of Tyron and Megan, but she was positive that they too, would grow up soon, and be reunited with her.

She nervously entered the townhouse, and for the first time in what felt like forever, she felt tranquility enter her heart. She hurriedly took her mobile phone from her purse, and dialed Ida's number at once.

Molly had made contact with Ida shortly before she had graduated, and even though she fruitlessly tried to contact Ryan, Ida informed her that he had left the country to study abroad, and that he had no intention of returning any time soon. It was at that moment that Molly was convinced that she had lost Ryan forever. She was sickened to discover that her life came to a halt the day she left Harper Valley for the very first time. Ida knew not to ask too many questions, but she often deliberated about what went so disastrously wrong between her two friends. Ida was abundantly conscious of the actuality that Molly still hopelessly adored Ryan. They all knew that a love like theirs didn't simply breathe its last breath out of the blue. She told Molly that while Ryan could never truthfully move on from her, he was capable of moving forward with his life, without her. By the time that Molly had moved to the city, Ida was contentedly settled into a blissful union with Louis. It was not long after their wedding that their delightful baby girl had made her entrance into the world. Ida had fallen pregnant in Grade Eleven. Both she and Louis were strong-willed in the decision to get married without hesitation. Louis had sustained his studies, while Ida wanted nothing more than to be a stay-at-home mom to her daughter.

"Ida?" Molly could barely control her enthusiasm. "Hey, you!" Ida was over the moon when she heard Molly's familiar voice. "I did it! I'm finally here!" "So, what are you waiting for? Come on over!" Ida almost insisted. "I'm exhausted, but I will pop in first thing in the morning! I just wanted to let you know that I made it!" Molly promised to drop in the next day before she hurriedly said goodnight. Turning to glance around her, she was ecstatic to experience utter liberation for the very first time in her life. She slowly climbed the stairs to what would soon become her new study, and she glanced around her while grinning from ear to ear. Molly dreamed of becoming a novelist since she was just a little girl, and with what was left of her trust fund, she could quite possibly spin it into a reality for her. She was indebted to Ida for overseeing the job of having all her furniture delivered and moved in on time. All that was left for her to do was to unpack her suitcases that were still bundled up in her car.

Molly took a long searing bath, and after climbing into bed, she gently stroked the ring that Ryan had once given her. "I wonder where you are today?" She whispered softly before drifting off to sleep.

It was just after nine the following morning when Molly knocked on Ida's front door. "Hey!" Ida breathlessly embraced Molly when she found her animatedly standing at her front door. Molly instantly caught a peek of the little girl that Ida was cradling in her arms. "Oh goodness, this must be Piper. She's beautiful, Ida." Molly instinctively took Piper from Ida's arms, sensitive to her tears that were callously shimmering in her eyes as she was unexpectedly reminded of her own baby, the baby she had murdered. The child she would never watch grow up, the baby that not a soul knew of. "Are you okay, Molly?" Ida was staggered to notice the tears roll down Molly's cheeks. "Oh, I'm fine. I'm just so happy to be here, and it is so good to see you. I've missed you. And who can't get emotional holding a baby in their arms?" She feebly offered as an explanation, hesitant to tell Ida of her baby, but certain that she remains cautious before blurting it all out. Ida would unquestionably disapprove of the outcome, and it was a detail that Molly was not yet courageous enough to deal with at that very instant.

She followed Ida into the kitchen where she found Louis who was geared up and ready to run off to the office. "Molly!" He leaned forward and kissed her on the cheek, "How are you?" Molly was thrilled to hear how pleased he was to see her again. "I'm fine, wow look at you!" Molly was inspecting every inch of Louis. "Yeah, the working man's life." He smiled timidly before he promptly left for work. "I'm so happy for you two." Molly was sincerely delighted for Ida and Louis, and entirely infatuated with Piper.

Molly and Ida met up virtually daily following their reunion, and subsequent to Molly moving into her new home. She grew increasingly emotionally over-involved with Piper, while continuing to hide the loss of her own child from Ida or Louis. She began writing manuscripts almost right away, as though it was something incredible that she had been engaged in for her entire life. When Molly successfully published her fourth novel, she had contentedly established a life that she could shape and tailor-make to suit her every need. Even though she never saw or heard from Ryan, Molly would frequently hear Louis discuss Ryan with Ida.

He had remained out of the country, and about to finalize his final year which was drawing to an end. Louis mentioned that although he had been presented with a brilliant offer for a position with an engineering firm abroad, Ryan was keen to return home, back to Murray Field. Louis was excited at the prospect of having his closest friend back home, but Molly felt her tummy turn each time he mentioned Ryan's name. Ida habitually and curiously snooped on information from Louis about who Ryan was dating, but Louis' answer on no account faltered, even once. He never dated seriously, and would go out with women, poles apart from each other, every other week. They giggled about this more often than not, but they would cautiously bear in mind that Molly was listening attentively.

Molly had become exceedingly affectionate towards Piper, and when she visited with Ida, she would as a rule, bath and feed Piper before putting her to bed. It became second nature to Molly to carry around the baby monitor, and Louis and Ida would regularly taunt her, and frequently inform her of the fact that Piper was awfully mystified as to who her actual mother was.

Alice VL

Molly

Louis refrained from telling Ida or Molly that Ryan's resolution to return to Murray Field was almost not going to come about when he discovered that Molly was back. When Louis told him that she had returned, he persistently requested information about Molly, and grew increasingly astringent, resulting in a disagreement essentially about her with almost each phone call. There were moments that Ryan became heated, and commanded Louis to never utter her name even once, and then there were moments that he begged his friend to tell him more about Molly. Louis never told Molly of their conversations, but he knew that his friend still held Molly dear, and that their love had devastatingly distorted him. Losing Molly was something that Ryan never adapted to. It was an overwhelming defeat that he failed to come to terms with. Louis silently prayed that their friends could in some way, find their way back to one other, and put an end to all the anguish that he detected in Molly's eyes, and heard in Ryan's voice.

Louis narrowly watched Molly and noticed the look in her eyes when he mentioned Ryan. He was desperate to ask her on numerous occasions what went wrong, but Ida constantly blocked him, perceptive to the fact that her friend was in no way at all, equipped to offer up an explanation just yet. At night, Ida and Louis would engage in discussions regarding their friends, and they both established without a doubt, that they still belonged together. They knew that something horrifying must have happened, yet, they were convinced that there was nothing Ryan and Molly couldn't work out. Ida was positive that it would be just a matter of time before they faced one another head on, and she prayed that that era would approach swiftly.

She noticed how Molly was growing depressed and emaciated as the days passed by, while at the same time, Louis mentioned on one occasion that it was as though Molly was fading little by little. Louis would habitually implore Ryan to call Molly, but he refused to even consider it. Ida in turn, tried desperately to persuade Molly to get in touch with Ryan, but she no longer knew how to. Molly had no clue of to how to carry on as though nothing had gone wrong between them. It was safer for her to keep her distance, and she prayed that in some way in the future, she might have the courage to face him again.

Alice VL

Molly

FACING THE PAST

Molly had just begun her fifth novel when her phone unexpectedly rang just before nightfall. "Hey!" Molly was pleased to hear Ida's composed voice. "Hi there. Listen, its Piper's 4th birthday on Saturday, and we wanted to check if you fancied coming over?" Ida clumsily and hurriedly invited Molly over for Piper's birthday party and get-together. "Of course, I haven't missed one birthday yet, why do you ask?" She was a tad bit perplexed that Ida was under the groundless impression that she would perhaps turn down an invitation to attend Piper's birthday celebrations. "Just asking. Just want to make sure you're coming. You know? Guests and such. Catering and such. Okay. See you then on Saturday!" Ida replied quickly before hanging up at once.

"Strange?" Molly thought as she gazed out through her study window that overlooked the ocean. "I always go?" Molly had the most breathtakingly beautiful views of the marine, and intermittently sat at her workstation staring out onto the ocean. She would sit until late at night reflecting on Ryan, her parents, Tyron and Megan. Although she longed for Ryan with every fraction of her heart, she could not pluck up the courage to ask

Louis for Ryan's number, more than anything, she failed to recognize that she possessed the clemency in her heart, to make contact with her parents again. Molly was nudged by the fact that she no doubt still adored her father, but she begrudged him for cutting her off from Ryan.

Alice VL

Molly

When she heedlessly strolled up to Ida's front door on the Saturday of Piper's birthday, Molly was caught off-guard by the number of guests they had invited that day, as opposed to the year before. Clutching Piper's gift in one hand, she opened the door with the other. "Aunty Molly!" Piper screeched when she recognized her. "Hey, birthday girl! Happy birthday, baby." Molly seized Piper in her arms and spun her around while performing a wretched version of 'Happy Birthday' to her. "I'm four!" Piper breathlessly exclaimed while attempting to tally her age off her fingers. "You're such a big girl now!" Molly giggled and kissed her on the cheek. Ida approached them with enormous urgency, frantic to take Piper from Molly's arms. "No!" Piper began to wail at once. "Oh, leave her!" Molly was insistent, content with carrying Piper around in her arms.

"She is exhausting. Anyways, come on outside. Louis and all the other guests are out there already." Ida turned around and led the way for Molly to follow. Something about Ida's demeanor convinced her that she was careful to avoid Molly. With confusion building up inside of her, she made her way outdoors to join Ida and Louis. She had just reached them, when she glanced around swiftly, realizing again the influx of guests that had been invited.

Molly had to look twice when her eyes caught a glimpse

Alice VL

of a face she had once known all too well, for far too long and for most of her life. She felt her legs grow frail, and her heart began to hammer fiercely when she noticed Ryan positioned on the other side of the pool. She realized too late that he had focused his awareness on her too. While she failed to perceive anyone else in the crowd, Molly wondered for just a split second whether her heart was misleading her.

Ryan was instantly responsive to Molly's presence, and seeing her again, took his breath away. She was as fragile as he could remember her to be, but her hair was longer and she appeared older even though in Ryan's mind, she was so much more beautiful than he could remember. Ryan could find no traces of the immature schoolgirl who had discarded him, and he was instantly distressed to realize that time had somehow tainted her. When he made his way towards her, Molly was convinced that her eyes were in no way, mendacious.

"Ryan?" She whispered nervously and for a split second, Molly was oblivious to the fact that she was holding Piper in her arms. The storm that had begun to assemble inside of her, reminded her of the utter reality that he was still accountable for her racing heart, and her twirling tummy. While staring into his reassuring and consoling eyes, she was confident that there were dissimilar details about him, something that impressed upon

Molly that he was not the boy she once left behind. Ryan had grown into the man she had imagined and anticipated he would, and although he had undeniably matured from the teenager she had left behind, she was certain that there were fundamentals about him that did not change, evolve or transform.

He gazed at her for what felt like forever, but instantly and unpredictably identified with her. Ryan noticed that the sparkle she owned some time ago was replaced by irrefutable sorrow, and he wondered at once where it had come from. "Hello Molly, Louis mentioned something about you being here today. It's good to see you again. You're still a sight for sore eyes, you know?" He paused to let out a faint, but bashful snigger. "How have you been?" He gently kissed her on her cheek, while instantaneously recognizing the scent of her skin. "I'm fine, thank you for asking. How are you?" She stumbled over her words, still stunned to find him there, all the while on tenterhooks by the possibility that he could hear the galloping of her heart. He smiled, defectively equipped to respond, but instantly conscious of the resentment that had begun to make its presence known to him. Molly calmed down slightly, uncertain of what to say next, before she abruptly turned to face Ida.

"Why didn't you tell me?" Molly felt abrupt irritation towards her friend, forcefully aware that she not prepared to find

Ryan there. "I wasn't sure he'd come." Ida replied frankly. For a moment, Molly felt at a complete loss for words for running into Ryan, but when she glanced back at him, she was reluctantly reminded that he was indubitably the one single man that she had been dreaming of. The only man that had the capability of enforcing a shudder throughout her entire body. It felt to her as though it was only yesterday that she saw him for the last time, but she was heartbroken to realize that time had passed them by. Ryan had walked away from her and made his way back to the other side of the pool. He knew that if he had stood watching her for only an instant longer, he would not be able to turn away from her again.

Louis cautiously approached Molly, and took Piper from her arms, "I'm glad you came." He smiled considerately, but desolately at her. "Can I get you something to drink?" "Oh, I, I rather want to go, Louis. I wasn't prepared for this, and I just feel a little out of place." She whispered quietly while realizing that she wouldn't be able to get through the day with Ryan so close to her. "I just came to wish Piper and bring her gift." "Come on Molly, its Piper's birthday. You usually give her a bath and put her to bed, more than ever on her birthday. She's not going to understand. Don't shun Ryan, please Molly?" Molly was positive that if she had left at that instant, it would be apparent to Ida, Louis, and Ryan that his attendance had inflicted restlessness on her, and she despised the idea of placing her friends in that position. "Fine, Louis, fine." She snorted tetchily before finding an open seat on the terrace.

Ryan gazed at her time and again, and when he noticed her sitting by herself, he had an overwhelming urge to be close to her. "Here, lemonade." She was appalled to find Ryan standing directly in front of her with two glasses in his hands. "Thanks." Molly took a glass from him before he tentatively sat in the open seat next to her. "So, are you here alone?" Molly lowered her head and desperately tried to focus on her glass. "Yes." "It's been a long time, you really look good, Mols." "It has been so long, yes. You look, you look good too, Ryan. You're exactly how I thought you'd turn out." Ryan smiled sadly, "So, Ida tells me that you're back permanently?" "Yes, I am. This is my home. I never belonged over there." Molly was vigilant on the issue of her parents. "How are your folks?" Molly looked away, unsure of how to respond. "Okay, I guess." Ryan grimaced and was unable to comprehend her response. "I, I don't have contact." Molly explained abruptly. Ryan wasn't sure what she meant, but instead of pressing her, he turned his awareness to Louis and Ida, attentive to the fact that she had no intention of discussing her parents, "Look at them. To think they have come this far, and everybody said it wouldn't work." "Yeah." Molly knew how complex it was for Ida and Louis to persuade their parents that they were all set and ready to get married. They swore to each parent that they knew what their responsibilities were, and that they would wrestle incessantly to make their nuptials work. After their initial shillyshallying, they reluctantly agreed to the union, and halfheartedly and unenthusiastically, sanctioned their marriage. She was swiftly reminded of her own father's response to the same circumstances and was immensely proud of Ida and Louis for never surrendering to pressure.

"That's always been my vision, you know? Oh right, you do know, but why am I telling you? It was never yours." Molly detected an insinuation of umbrage in his voice. She struggled to look him in the eye, while surrendering to the fact that he was right, but at the same time, responsive to the truth that all that was once upon a time good between them, was spoilt and irreparable. She single-handedly was answerable for all that had gone wrong between her and Ryan. Ryan was eager for an explanation from her for what precisely had taken place between them, but by the expression on her face, he was intensely conscious of the fact that she had not much to say to him. "Ryan."

They spent what was left of the day fiercely attempting to steer clear of one another, each of them sensing that the silence between them had made them both agonizingly uncomfortable. There was so much that Molly wanted to say to

Ryan, but there was so much more that she wanted to know from him. Her heart and her intellect swore to her that the moment they had found themselves in, was not the appropriate time for them to be having the conversation she had hoped they would never have, so instead, she stole glances from him every opportunity she had.

Ryan was engrossed in conversation with Louis. He told him about his stay abroad, but he conceded to the fact that he was relieved to be back. At one stage, Molly overheard him telling Louis that there was someone incredible in his life again, and while he was hardly confident as to where it would lead, he was enthusiastic about taking a chance with her. "I really like her, Louis." "If she makes you happy, buddy?" Louis had a nudging feeling that Ryan was fooling himself. "She's smart, beautiful, loyal and successful, what more does a guy want?" Louis smiled but could barely shake the feeling of discomfort by what Ryan was saying. "Yeah, but do you love her?" "We've just started dating, buddy but yes, I think so?" He unpredictably questioned his response to Louis, as though he needed to hear it out loud in order to believe it. Louis was convinced that Ryan was being deceitful to himself but was satisfied to learn that his friend had something to look forward to once again.

It aggrieved Molly to consider that Ryan felt nothing for

her any longer, that he was smitten with someone new, and when he approached her with another glass of lemonade, Molly abruptly excused herself. "I've got to get Piper bathed." She snapped before she picked Piper up and carried her into the house. Glancing at the clock in the hallway, Molly was crestfallen when she realized that it had only just turned seven thirty, and that the sun had no intention of setting any time soon, but Piper was exhausted and delighted to have her bath before sundown. After promptly sponging her down, Molly hurriedly dressed her before she laid her down on her bed and snuggly tucked her in. Piper took Molly's face into her hands, "I love you, aunty Molly." She whispered sleepily before drifting off almost at once.

Molly lingered while gazing at Piper for a while longer, furtively yearning for her own baby, wondering at the same time, who he or she might have resembled. Molly gently retrieved the baby monitor, before she turned to leave Piper's bedroom. "She's beautiful." Ryan appeared in the doorway of Piper's bedroom as Molly was about to leave. "Yes, she is." She glanced back at the little girl dead to the world, and secretly wondered how long he had been standing there while modestly unnerved by him.

As she brushed past him, Ryan grabbed her by her arm, "I can't do this, Molly. I can't pretend that nothing is going on here. Talk to me, what happened? Why didn't you come back? What happened to you in Park Hill? I just want to know, that's all." Molly was suddenly overcome with fear, unsure of how to explain away their lost years. "Not now, Ryan." She at once freed herself from his grip, convinced that she was powerless to deal with him at that very moment. Ryan had had enough of the façade. He needed answers from Molly, and he was determined that she gives him the answers he had been searching for, for years. "Now, Molly! I just need to; I have to know. I will never be a nuisance to you again, but just tell me!" He steadfastly grabbed a hold of both her arms. "Not here." "Fine, let's go for a walk on the beach then." While making their way over to the terrace, Ryan came to an abrupt halt when he faced Louis, "Louis, listen, we're going for a walk on the beach. Piper's asleep." He took the monitor from Molly and handed it over to Louis, with no intention of offering an appropriate explanation.

Louis nodded his head, and for an instant, wondered whether they had argued. He was abundantly aware of how misplaced his friend was without Molly, and he prayed that somehow, they could work through their issues, and perhaps, just possibly, they could work out the disputes between them. He knew how profoundly Ryan once loved her, and he had no doubt that Molly still cherished Ryan. Each time Molly's eyes glimmered, it was when he spoke of Ryan. A little voice inside of

Molly

him continually nudged him to a reality that Molly saying goodbye to Ryan, was a choice that was never hers, and for a reason other than no longer loving him. He watched them walk away and prayed one more time that they would find their way back to one another.

They walked in silence while keeping a secure distance from one another. When they reached the shore, Ryan disconsolately turned to Molly, "Tell me, Molly, did you really just stop loving me? Just like that? Did you really just give yourself to someone else?" "Ryan, please, it was so long ago." She tried to steer clear of all of his gratuitous questions while utterly convinced that she could never, unveil the truth to Ryan. "It's not that long ago, Molly! Because you see, I don't think you just stopped loving me. You still wear the ring around your neck, I saw it earlier." He wrathfully exposed the necklace from under her sweater. It was when he handed her first glass of lemonade earlier that day, that he noticed the ring. A moment he had established the certainty that there was more to their severance than Molly allegedly falling in love with someone else. Molly was stunned, unsure of what to say next. She lowered her head before she had begun to whimper unexpectedly. "I waited for you. I thought you loved me. Why did you leave me like that?" Molly grabbed Ryan by his arm, "I *did* love you, Ryan, but you never answered your phone! My dad took my phone away, and then I secretly tried to call you, but you never answered. You never even wrote me, nothing!" She paused to take in a deep breath, "You were meant to come after me! You were supposed to come for me!" Ryan was aware of the sorrow and extreme anxiety in her voice. He wasn't quite making sense of what Molly was saying, "I tried calling you after, but I just got your voicemail. I didn't think you'd give up on me so easily. What do you mean, come after you?" He was baffled all of a sudden and was desperate to make sense of her mumblings.

Molly was instantly aware of the fact that he was surprised, and at the same time, mystified by what she was saying, however, she had no way of impressing upon him the worst day of her life. "What are you saying here, Molly?" He was frantic to find the answers in her eyes. "I don't know what I'm saying, Ryan. I've said too much already." Ryan frowned when he noticed her fear and desperation. "Come with me, I want to show you something." He gently took her by her hand, before leading her back to Ida and Louis' house. When they reached Ida, Ryan intolerantly turned to her, "Listen, please tell Louis that I've, we've got to go. I'll call him tomorrow, okay?" Molly grabbed her purse before she followed Ryan to their cars. "Get in." He irately ordered after opening the passenger door for her. "I'll meet you there." "No. I'll bring you back, just get in the car, Molly. I'm not taking that chance that you might just drive off, and away again."

Molly

Molly climbed into the passenger seat before Ryan closed the door behind her. He slid into the driver's seat and pulled out of the driveway without saying another word. When they reached his home, Molly was stunned to realize that they were living in close proximity of one another. She was saddened to realize that they were both breathing in the same air, under the say moon, and below the same stars for a while, and they didn't even know it.

He switched off his car and signaled for her to follow him. Molly glanced around swiftly, and realized that he too, owned glorious views of the ocean. She followed brusquely behind him when he made his way into his bedroom, "Over here, Molly." He called out for her to join him. He retrieved a minute timber container from his closet and handed it to Molly. She nervously sat down on his bed and was unpredictably terrified of opening it. "Open it." Molly lifted the cover, and what she saw instantly took her breath away. There were dozens of unopened letters he had written her that were returned to him. By the date stamps, Molly realized that he had written her habitually, and with trembling hands, she began to read the first letter. Tears filled her eyes as she read on, unable to put them down. She fretfully gazed up at Ryan and noticed that his own tears were brimming in his eyes.

Alice VL

"I thought, I thought we had a plan, Molly?" He took a letter from her hand. "I didn't know what to do? I called your dad …" Molly was horrified to hear that Ryan had called her dad, and he never once told her that Ryan hadn't so easily, given up on her. "What about my dad?" "He alleged that you had met someone else, and that …" Molly was revolted by what her father had told him, and interrupted him without delay, "No, Ryan, no! I *loved* you, and I survived just to get back to you. I was crushed because of you! There was no one else, I swear. There has never been anyone else since you, since us. Everything that happened, was so that I could come home, and be with you again. I never got those letters, I *swear*." She was at once intensely exasperated as she recalled all that she was compelled to suffer and endure, and how exhaustingly she battled for their love. She was once again reminded of her father's brutality, and she was devastatingly mindful of how harshly he had punished her and Ryan for their one mistake.

"He said that you didn't want to see me again, that there was someone else?" Ryan struggled to find the words while swallowing back on a restricting bulge in his throat. "Why would he say that if it weren't true, Molly? I don't understand it, so please, just explain it to me! Nothing makes sense. None of this feels right?" Molly knew that irrespective of how hard she tried to banish him from her heart and eject him from her mind, Ryan would for all eternity be, the only man to lay a claim to her heart. The only way in which to compel Ryan to undoubtedly believe that she still loved him, that she would have given her life for him, was to expose the truth about all that had gone off-track, and all that she had done. "It was complicated, Ryan. My dad, he wouldn't let me speak to you. I was, I came back after that last holiday and I was, pregnant, and ..." She was instantly unconfident of how to accurately explain about the baby before Ryan interrupted her, "What? You were pregnant?" The bewilderment and perplexity were unmistakably present in his voice as he stumbled over his words. "Molly? What happened? You had a baby?" He grabbed her by her shoulders. "No, I wanted to tell you, Ryan. No, I had, an abortion, and then afterwards, I didn't know how to tell you! And when enough time had passed, I never wanted you to know." While listening to her version of the truth, and the reality that she had massacred their child, he was hauntingly aware of the fact that she had said too much. He felt repulsion and abhorrence make its way into his heart, and as he witnessed her brutal weeping, he felt no mercy for her. Ryan was desperate to injure her in the way he had been wounded by her. He was frantic for her to feel the soreness that he was sensitive to at that very moment. Molly had begun shuddering uncontrollably while Ryan simply turned away from her.

"You would never do that. How could you, Molly?" Ryan

still could not believe that it was something Molly would have gone thought with. "I, I'm sorry, Ryan. My dad ..." "He *made* you do it? No, Molly, *you* made that choice, only you! You could've come to me; you executed our child! You took away everything! I never in the slightest imagined you could do something like that! You always said you could never go through with something like that, you once said it was an assassination on a human life, do you even remember that?" He raised his voice, lacking complexity in considering the sequence of events that had taken place at a particular point in time. Molly was trampled by his lashing out at her, but she reluctantly acknowledged that it was justly reasonable for him to counter in that manner. She ought to have tried harder to keep their baby. She should have waged a war between her and her father, but she repentantly lacked the audacity to stand up to him.

Molly got up from his bed and turned to run off from his bedroom before she came to a screeching halt. "I wanted to tell you! I tried! I, I'm sorry, Ryan. I don't know what else to say to you? I didn't know what else to do!" Ryan grabbed her arm furiously, "I will never, in no way *ever*, forgive you for this, Molly. Let me take you back to your life, and you know what? I am relieved that I am not in it anymore!" She witnessed the devastating truth of Ryan turning his back on her. She had no right to hold him accountable for walking away from her. She had deceived their love, and nothing she could say or do could alter what had happened all those years ago, but at the same time, she was not ready, or in any way, geared up to let go of him just yet.

"Ryan, please just hear me out!" When he turned back to face her, Molly noticed that his tears were rolling unreservedly down his cheeks. "There is nothing you can say to me Molly, absolutely nothing! I loathe you! No, wait. I would have to feel something for me to despise you, but there is *nothing*!" He snapped back at her before he finally led the way out to his car. They walked in silence while Ryan's heart convinced him that he could never exonerate Molly for what she had done.

While driving back to Ida and Louis' home, Ryan stared directly ahead of him, and sat in a ghostly silence. Molly glanced at him over and over again and was once again vigilant of the fact that the anguish of losing Ryan, hadn't at all improved, or became easier as an adult. Her heart reminded her of how acutely she still loved Ryan, even though she had lost him once again. Molly wasn't sure that she would survive losing Ryan again, yet she pitifully prayed that he would find it in his heart to empathize with the position she was forced into, but most of all, to absolve her for her reprehensible transgression someday.

He pulled up next to her car, and immediately looked the other way, stubbornly avoiding eye contact with her. "Ryan, please! I came back for you." She whispered, almost afraid of her own voice, but desperate to tell Ryan that she did all that was humanely possible to find her way back to him, to find her way back home. "Just go, Molly! I can't even stand the sight of you. You're just a little speck too late!"

Ryan hastily drove off without looking back in the rear-view mirror. It frustrated him that he allowed her to have such an uncompromising effect on him once again, even after all the years apart from one another. Ryan ultimately understood what had come to pass between them, and he was irrevocably cognizant that the uncertainty that had loitered between them, had finally been resolved. His heart instructed him to let go of her while bullying him into believing that Molly never loved him at all. He was distraught over what she had done, and for a moment, Ryan wished to a certain extent, that there was in truth, another man that she was in love with, precisely as her father had told him. It would be simpler to overcome dealing with a new love, than to admit to her duplicity.

When Molly entered her home, she scampered directly into her bedroom, and collapsed onto her bed, weeping inconsolably for Ryan. She snatched the ring from her neck and allowed it plunge onto the floor and roll out into the darkness. It was of no significance or importance to her any longer. She believed in all earnest that Ryan would return to her, but the repugnance she witnessed in his eyes earlier was something that Molly had never seen prior to that day, and she was sure that it was an expression she in no way sought to willingly absorb again.

Her phone rang in the darkness, but Molly left it to ring, frantic to shut out one and all. Turning her thoughts to her parents, Molly knew that she couldn't loathe them anymore than she did at that very second, and amnesty was nowhere near an option for them. She thought of Ryan again, it was all she could cogitate. She thought about the boy she had fallen hopelessly in love with as a child, and later as a teenager again, and who undertook to take care of her. They had equally broken the promises they lovingly made to one another. A life without Ryan would be one of her most awful fears come true. "I'm so sorry, Ryan." She whispered softly before drifting off to sleep.

It was long after midnight when Ryan pulled up at Louis and Ida's home after indulging in a number of alcoholic refreshments at their neighborhood pub. "You okay, buddy?" Louis recognized the fact that Ryan had a large amount to drink, and even though he was not quite inebriated, he was clearly not sober either. Ida aided Louis while they accompanied Ryan indoors, before she hurriedly turned to make her way into the kitchen. Ryan collapsed onto their sofa and buried his head in his hands. "Ryan, buddy, what happened?" Louis affectionately placed his hand on Ryan's shoulder.

"She got pregnant, Louis. That last holiday, Molly got pregnant." Louis took a seat on the sofa next to Ryan and could hardly believe a word of what he was hearing. "Molly had a baby?" Louis questioned him in disbelief. Ida walked in and stared incredulously at Louis. "Ryan, did Molly have a baby?" She sat down on the coffee table across from Ryan. Ryan gazed up at her, his eyes red and inflamed. "No." He mumbled, hesitant to inform his dearest friends of what Molly had done. "I don't understand, Ryan?" Ida was thoroughly puzzled by Ryan's mutterings. "She got pregnant the last time she was here, and, and she had an abortion when she went back home." The tears were rolling violently down his cheeks once more. Ida placed her arms around him and was summarily quailed to find him so entirely inconsolable. "Molly wouldn't, she would never? Molly would never do that. She loved you Ryan, and she left so many messages for you?" Ida tried to make sense of it all while at the same time, doing her utmost to reason with Ryan. "She did, Ida. Oh yes, she did, and those messages, probably just to torture me with." He at once rose to his feet before he turned away from them. Ryan sneered miserably and waved goodbye, before making his way back to his car. Louis walked his friend out, and when they reached the car, he turned back to Louis. "And then she said she loved me?" The cynicism was unmistakable in his tone of voice but was instantly broken when Ryan burst out laughing. Louis felt colossal pity for his friend, and finally understood his antagonism. While Louis strolled back into his home, he questioned whether any of them ever knew Molly at all.

Alice VL

TRAPPED IN YESTERDAY

Molly awoke to the reverberation of a hammering at her front door. When she glanced over at her alarm clock, she noticed that it was after eleven in the morning. "Was I asleep the whole time?" She was staggered for a moment and could barely identify with why she had slept as long as she did before she hurriedly made her way down the passageway. "Ida?" Garbled in perplexity, she gazed at her friend stationed at her front door. "Where's Piper?" Molly promptly glanced around for her. "She's with Louis." Ida brushed past Molly, and swiftly made her way into to the kitchen. "So, Molly, what exactly happened yesterday, with Ryan?" Ida poured Molly a cup of coffee. Molly gaped at Ida and recalled the events of the previous night. "He hates me." She lowered her head, unable to look Ida in the eye. "Yeah well, you can't blame him." Molly began to sob again, before she repentantly turned away from Ida, incapable of looking at her.

"You know? He told you?" Molly felt her heart sting. "Ryan came back drunk last night. He was falling all over the place

Alice VL

telling Louis that you murdered his child, that you had an abortion. Is that true? Did you?" Molly was mortified by her actions, but so much more ashamed of being unable to stand up to her father. "Yes." Molly hunched her head, perceptive to the fact that she could no longer continue with the propaganda. Ida shook her head irately, "How could you, Molly?"

"Will you just stop crucifying me!" Molly hollered out before she hurled her coffee mug against the wall, leaving it to shatter into a thousand pieces. "If it's not Ryan, it's you!" Ida was horrified by Molly's sudden burst of anger and bent down to gather up the broken pieces. "You know Molly, I fell pregnant in grade eleven when I was just seventeen, but Louis was there for me. He didn't abandon me. We loved each other, and we wanted to get married. My parents were totally against us, but we stood together, and we stood by each other. You and Ryan loved each other too, so none of this makes sense to me? I always thought that nothing could ever come between you guys, nothing. I mean, at school, you guys were always making plans. Isn't that what you guys wanted, to get married as soon as you graduated? Why did you do it? How did it all change? I just don't understand what was so bad in your life that made you do it?"

"It doesn't matter, anymore Ida." Molly no longer wanted to explain, while vigorously swabbing at the tears on her cheeks. "Molly, we've been friends forever and I love you, but I thought I knew you. I thought you loved Ryan, and I truly believed that you guys could get through anything?" "You do know me, Ida! You've known me since we were kids. I tried! I begged my father, but he wouldn't listen. I begged my mother, and she wouldn't listen either! He wanted to send me away, and I knew, I knew if I didn't do it, he would never let me see Ryan again! Is that what you want to hear, how pathetic I was? My dad forced me to do it and, I feel like I didn't have a say in anything! I loved Ryan more than anything. Do you think I'd want to slaughter our baby? I just didn't have a say, and I tried so hard to oppose him, and fight against it. It was for nothing! It was for nothing!" Molly had become hysterical. "Afterwards, I just never had the heart to tell him, or you. I didn't know how to? My heart was so broken, and I just wanted to run away, and come home, but I had to wait." Molly babbled while feeling as though a floodgate of tears had opened up inside of her.

"I wanted my baby! I wanted Ryan's baby, Ida! I wanted to hold onto it and onto our love. In my heart, I knew that our child would somehow keep us together, forever, and no matter how far apart we were." She collapsed to her knees in desolation while sobbing ferociously. "Every time I look at Piper, I think of my baby, and I feel dead inside. When I close my eyes, I can hear him cry." Ida placed her arms around Molly. "I'm so sorry, Molly.

Molly

I didn't know. I should have listened first. Did you tell Ryan the whole story?" "He won't listen, he won't. He can't even look at me." "Well try harder, Molly. You owe him that." Ida got up, and gazed down at Molly, "Listen Molly, you should've just told him. Your dad couldn't stop you from telling him." "But he did, Ida. I tried to, Ida. How many times didn't I ask you to tell Ryan to take my call? How many times? Remember? How many times?" Molly shouted out feverishly. Ida turned away from her, unable to fact her, admitting to the fact that Molly had tried endlessly to speak to Ryan.

"Listen, I have to go, Louis must get back to work, but Piper wants you over for dinner tonight, will you come? We can talk some more tonight, all right?" Molly sighed. Dinner and company were the last thing on her mind, yet, her loneliness was suddenly haunting her. "Yeah, sure."

Alice VL

Molly

Climbing out of the shower, Molly resentfully acknowledged that Ryan would not at all pardon her, or begin to grasp what she was going through, just as Ida initially refused to understand. She deceived him, and there was nothing in the world that she could think of to validate or explain why she allowed her father to intimidate her to such a degree. Molly felt yet again that she had lost Ryan, and the time had finally presented itself to her, to bury the pestering past, and carry on without him. It was time to bring an end to her incessant dwelling on the love that they had once shared for one another and pick up the shattered pieces even though she was plagued by a wearisome impression that Ryan will forever live actively in her heart. There would constantly be reminders of yesteryear, and the barrenness she felt inside would relentlessly remind her of the baby she and Ryan could and should have treasured.

Louis stopped by Ryan's place on the spur of the moment, enroute to work, enabling him to check in on his friend. Ryan had just climbed out of the shower when Louis discovered that he had calmed down and seemed more or less normal again. "Listen buddy, why don't you come over for dinner tonight? We can talk some more?" Louis was zealously aware of the fact that Ida had invited Molly over for dinner that evening. "I don't want to talk about Molly anymore, Louis. What's done is done, and what's over is over, but I'd love to come over for one of Ida's home cooked meals" Ryan patted his friend on the back before Louis said a swift goodbye and left for work.

When Molly arrived for dinner, Louis was the one to welcome her at the front door. "Hey!" He noticed at once that her eyes were red and puffed-up. "You okay?" He took her coat from her. "Yeah, I'm fine." She instantly and unwittingly let out a forced smile. "Listen Mols, just give Ryan some time. Ida told me what happened, and when she put it to me that way, it made more sense, knowing your dad. I just don't think Ryan sees it like that, but how could he if no-one tells him, right?" Molly nodded her head in silence, while wanting to shout out that he would never listen anyway. "Aunty Molly!" Piper yelled before leaping into Molly's arms. "Hello baby girl." Molly chuckled before placing kisses all over her face until Piper giggled hysterically.

"Uncle Ryan and Aunty Flo are also here." Piper blurted out animatedly. Molly turned questioningly to Louis when he realized that she had no comprehension of who 'Aunty Flo' was. "Flo, she's with Ryan." "Hey! You made it!" Ida joined them in the dining room, and took Piper from Molly. "Let me introduce you, Flo this is Molly, Molly, this is Flo." Molly was sure that her heart would shatter into smithereens when she grasped the fact that Ryan had introduced Flo to their friends. She smiled halfheartedly at her and realized at once how entirely dissimilar they were. She towered above Molly, hauling a mane of long dark curls while sporting striking blue eyes. Bluer than Molly had ever laid her eyes on, but she was sure that if she stared long enough, they would turn white. For a second, Molly felt enormously unadorned next to her, and unexpectedly became insecure and terrifyingly uncomfortable.

Ryan was satisfyingly responsive of her reaction to Flo and presumed instantly exactly how Molly was feeling. He felt enormous respite at witnessing the extent of how precisely apprehensive Molly had become around Flo. It convinced him that she had retained undeniable feelings for him. Ryan discovered her reaction as an opening to insult Molly, almost as dreadfully as she had once snubbed him. He felt an unforeseen twinge in his heart simply by the notion of distressing her, but his mind convinced him that Molly ought to be forced to experience the devastation he felt only a short while ago and punished accordingly.

He turned to Flo, and kissed her delicately, effusively alert to the fact that Molly was secretly scrutinizing the pair. He eagerly hoped that it ripped into her heart, just as her words of the day before had sliced into his. "Let's eat!" Ida unnervingly tried to slice through the abrupt awkwardness when Louis carried in the food. "Come, sit by me." Flo signaled to Piper. "I want to sit by my Aunty Molly." Piper made her way to the empty seat adjacent to Molly. "So, Molly, Ryan said you guys used to date at school?" Flo was eager to engage in conversation with Molly. "How funny that sounds now, right? It was a really long time ago." Molly giggled nervously, wanting Ryan to take note of her supposed detachment of him. "What happened?" Molly was staggered by Flo's candor, and by no means quite knew how to simplify the fact that she had lost the man of her destiny, the only man she would ever love. "Oh wait, let me tell you!" Ryan brusquely interrupted when he detected how red and puffy Molly's eyes still were. "We just weren't that into each other. The end, plain and simple." With a mystifying heart, he was unpredictably anxious to spare her the degradation of the truth, but at the same time, he was frantic to disgrace her. It was an ongoing battle inside of him, torn between defending her, and crushing her. Ryan knew the line between the two were so thin, and he spent too much time hopping around between the two.

Louis and Ida glared at one another while undoubtedly mindful of Ryan's perjury. Once dinner was dished up in complete and uncomfortable silence, Ryan once again turned to face Molly. He tried to remain silent, but his core would no longer allow him, "Flo and I were deliberating earlier, Molly. Maybe you can help, what is your position on abortion?" Ryan was frenetic for the answers his heart found so agonizingly necessary. Molly just about stifled when she grasped the position Ryan was placing her in, and urgently tried to keep the tears that had begun to shimmer in her eyes, from escaping. "Ryan!" Louis furiously attempted to silence his friend. "No, honestly, I *want* to know. I *want* to hear Molly's opinion. I've just recently heard she is a pro." "Come on, Ryan." Ida tried to rescue her friend from enduring anymore distress. Ryan was certain that Molly was in agony. He was convinced that she had been crying non-stop. Her eyes told him a thousand tales of hurt and despondence. He knew that inviting Flo along to dinner would instigate a kind of destruction, that would cause her world to come to an absolute stand still, but Ryan was committed and eager to press on. He hunted her soul and wouldn't surrender until he had clutched her broken heart into his bare hands. For Ryan, crushing her heart alone was barely passable, it was crucial that she suffer. He desperately wanted to witness her endure ruthless anguish, but more than that, he was anxious for her to be see his wounds and force her to identify with the fact that she alone was accountable for his utter desolation while acknowledging the reality that she had turned her back on him. "Come on, Molly, you're the expert here. Tell us, do you think a woman has any privileges over another life inside of her?"

Molly calmly placed her knife and fork back on her plate before she once again gulped down on the well-known and inexhaustible lump in her throat. She had in no way before, ever witnessed Ryan act in such a cold-blooded manner. She was vividly sensitive to the awful truth that Ryan was launching a sadistic assault on her. The love that Ryan had for her, and once boasted with, had vanished, and the time had come for Molly to acknowledge his fury. "I, no, Ryan. I have never thought that and have always been pro-life. You *know* that? I don't think that a woman has the right to decide whether her child should live or die, and I have never thought that. God alone decides whether a baby is born into this world, or not. It's just, sometimes, when you're still a little girl …" She embarked on presenting a courageous effort to defend herself before Ryan curtly interrupted her. "Bullshit! There are no excuses, no matter what. Every woman has the right to decide what happens! Even a teenager, Molly. Your pro-life bullshit makes no sense here!" "Are you crying, Aunty Molly?" Piper was entirely disturbed to find Molly in tears.

"No, my eyes are burning, sweetie." Molly bravely attempted a halfhearted smile for Piper. It was apparent to Ryan that Flo was baffled by his resentment, and she found it complex to ascertain how Molly was integrated into Ryan's acrimony. She made an effort to grapple with where his animosity was born from, but the longer she listened to him, the less she understood. "So, listen, honey?" Ryan turned to face Flo squarely in the eye,

Molly

"Hypothetically speaking, you were seventeen, and pregnant with my baby. We are in a long, long, *very* long-term relationship. We are allegedly in love, and we've made all these wonderful plans for our future together. Say, I gave you an engagement ring, and swore to marry you after we've known each other our entire lives. You *know* I will support you, no matter what happens, what would you do?" Flo hugged her glass of wine before she turned to Ryan. "Nothing. I would probably do what Ida and Louis did, get married and start a life together." She sipped at her wine while still deep in thought, "But, and this is a big but, I would *never* have an abortion. I love you, and I'd love our baby, no matter what. I'd want to hold on to that, hold onto you, does that make sense?" Louis and Ida glanced over at Ryan, who was shooting undetectable daggers at Molly while attentively listening to what Flo was saying. "You know Ryan, things aren't always as black and white as it seems." Louis did his best to halt the attack on Molly. "Oh yeah, Louis? So, tell me, my friend, what justifies an abortion? What? I really want to know. Enlighten me then." Molly explicitly understood at once that Ryan would mercilessly punish her for what she had done, and from the innermost part of her, she was ardently aware that his behavior was entirely reasonable and understandable. Turning back to Ryan, Molly glared at him, and detected utter revulsion in his eyes. It was an expression she was single-handedly answerable for, and she was not once able to anticipate that Ryan would be capable of the abhorrence she saw in his eyes. "You know, Ryan, sometimes a girl of seventeen can't depend on her guy to stand by her. Sometimes she can't fight everyone on her own!"

"How can he if she doesn't give him a chance! How must he if she doesn't even tell him! The only thing she tells him is that she doesn't want to see him again!" Ryan's rage had reached a new high when Flo suddenly realized how ignorant she had been throughout the entire debate. "Ryan?" Ryan quickly took Flo's hand in his, "Sorry." "No Ryan, what is going on here?" Flo fleetingly glimpsed at Molly. Molly was entirely conscious of Flo's state of perplexity due to their disagreement, but she had no idea of how to put an end to it. Ryan dropped his knife and fork and turned back to Molly. "Ask Molly." Flo's eyes trailed searchingly over at Molly. "Molly, what have you got to do with all this?" Flo was bemused by the abrupt conflict that had made its presence known between Ryan and Molly. Molly bowed her head and was once again mortified by her past. "Oh Ryan, let it go." Ida was desperate to put an end to the quarrelling. "Molly, poor little Molly girl couldn't stand up to daddy, and ran away from me. She had an abortion, you know?" Ryan clarified his sullenness as swiftly as he was able to.

Flo turned to Molly while unreservedly stunned by what

Ryan had alleged only a moment ago. "She didn't even have the decency, not even an ounce of decency to tell me, or to give me a chance to work it out with her or her father. No! Molly made all the decisions!" He temporarily suspended his attack on her to gulp down the last mouthful of his wine, "You could've given me the baby, Molly, at least it would've stood a chance." "Ryan." Louis placed his hand empathetically on his friend's shoulder, "It was a long time ago. Let it go." "Really?" Ryan had remained overwhelmingly exasperated. "Do you know that the baby would've been Piper's age?" He paused just long enough to glance at Piper, "Do you know how that makes me feel, sitting here, seeing her with Piper and knowing, *knowing* what she did? She's a fake, Louis! Pretending to love Piper so much and yet, she butchers her own child. What kind of a con artist is she?"

Molly felt the agonizing and excruciating hammering in her heart once again whilst listening to what Ryan was declaring. Her mind reprimanded her, and confirmed that Ryan was right while she too, repeatedly reflected on her own baby when she looked at Piper. Her baby would have been the same age as Piper, but she would never get to hold him, or by no means get to hold her in her arms. Molly lifted her eyes to face Ryan.

The crowd grew silent, and the world could hear a pin drop when no-one as much as breathed. They were hauntingly responsive to the tears that were brimming mercilessly in her eyes. "Don't you think I don't think about that, Ryan? Every time, every *single* time I hold Piper in my arms, I think, and I wonder. I *do* love Piper, damn it, Ryan. Don't you think that I think about what I've done every day of my life? And wish, *pray* that I could somehow turn back the time? Do you think it hasn't changed me? Even though you don't believe me, I didn't choose it Ryan, but I *hate* myself for it. I hate me so much, and right now, I hate you too. I wish I never met you! I wish I never came back here!"

Molly could barely take another verbal beating from Ryan. When he detected the anxiety and shudder in her voice, Ryan was instantly remorseful for what he had said. He was so sure that he would feel better, but his attack on her only made him feel shoddier. He almost unswervingly regretted the assault on her, even though he could hardly refrain from challenging her. Ryan gawked at Molly, anxious to seize her in his arms, and beg her for forgiveness, but his heart reminded him that it was too late. The damage he had inflicted on her, were wounds he could never retract or excuse, instead he lowered his head before he picked up his knife and fork and scoffed in silence.

"I can't do this." Turning to Ida and Louis, Molly was exasperated at once, "You should've told me he was going to be here." She swallowed back on the tears that were threatening to silence her, and turned to Flo, "Please excuse me. I am leaving. I? I am truly sorry for what happened here tonight, Flo, and I am so sorry we had to meet like this. I really, really wish you both well." Molly got up to her feet at once. "Aunty Molly, you didn't bath me?" Piper tearfully reminded Molly that she routinely bathed her and put her to bed when she came over. "Yes, Aunty Molly, you haven't bathed her yet." Ryan echoed with a hint of mockery before sipping on a newly poured glass of wine, still powerless to control his temper. "Ryan, what's the matter with you?" Flo snubbed before turning to Piper, "I'll bath you if you want?" She cheerfully offered as an alternative. "I want Aunty Molly to bathe me." Piper lamented while clutching weepily at Molly's hand. "Alright, let's go." Molly lifted Piper in her arms and carried her to the bathroom.

While bathing Piper, Molly allowed her tears to roll without restraint down her cheeks once again. Ryan had ruthlessly crushed her heart over and over again, and yet, the torment was in no way subsiding. Molly was devastatingly aware that Ryan's rage had grown daily as the days went on, and she was convinced that his resentment towards her was assassinating her at a snail's pace. "If only I could go back." Molly thought to herself, mindful of the fact that she could by no means ever, turn back the clock. "Come on, let's get you to bed." Molly hugged Piper after dressing her into her warm and snug night clothes before she carried her into her bedroom. "Piper, I love you so much. Don't ever forget that, okay? And don't you ever listen to anyone tell you otherwise." Molly covered her gently before placing her teddy bear next to her. When she realized that Piper had fallen asleep, Molly dabbed at her tears, and turned to leave.

She was staggered to unexpectedly find Ryan standing in the doorway. She couldn't deny or discard the sorrow in his eyes. "This could've been us, Molly. It was part of what we planned. It was what we've always wanted, remember?" He whispered in a trembling voice before he made way for her to pass him, while gazing at Piper without making another sound.

"Thanks for dinner guys. Bye Flo, nice meeting you, and again, I am truly sorry about tonight." Molly courageously lifted her hand to wave before turning to leave.

Ryan walked back into the dining room abruptly after Molly had left and sat down beside Flo once again. Ida and Louis were both wholeheartedly aware of the fact that Ryan was wrecked inside. Flo took Ryan's hand and squeezed it gently, perceptive to the notion that Ryan was carrying around an implausible amount of hurt and anguish for the loss of his child. Ryan could not banish Molly and the wretchedness in her eyes from his mind. He was sincerely repentant for all he had accused

Molly

her of, and he hoped that he could somehow make amends with her someday.

Alice VL

Molly

Molly marched straight into her study when she finally reached her home. She dolefully sat down behind her desk and gazed out over the ocean. It was the end of a day that had been far too challenging for her heart to deal with. She was comfortable and at ease with being on her own, and away from Ryan. The weather had become miserable, but it was nothing that could quantify the way she felt inside. She stared desolately at the portrait of Ryan on her desk, and she questioned how she would ever have the ability to endure seeing him with another woman time and again. Her heart ached for him, and regardless of how enormously she struggled to, she could not get the impression of detestation in his eyes, out of her mind. The one person that she felt sheltered by, the only person she relied on was moreover the very same person that instigated a frightening, and unrelenting assault on her heart. He was hurting too, but she was convinced that he had no intention of giving her an opportunity to right all her wrongs with him ever again. Her mind wandered once more to a point in time when they were merely children. "I love you Molly, forever." He habitually assured her, "I will always be there for you, and it doesn't matter what you do."

Molly was entirely distracted while profoundly in thought when she heard a deliberate thud at her front door. She hurriedly made her way downstairs while glancing at the clock against the wall. "Eleven thirty?" Molly was not at all equipped

Alice VL

for the vision that appeared to her at her front door. She was certain that an invisible dagger was sadistically and relentlessly piercing through her heart. While standing motionlessly and in a daze, Molly realized that she had involuntarily begun inhaling shorter breaths. "Ryan?" She shamefully gazed at him while he stood outside in the shadows of the darkness. She prayed that he his presence was not in any way, a crucifying repeat of all she had failed in, and disappointed him with. Molly no longer had the vigor to thrash out their differences with him, and for an instant, for just a moment, she acutely regretted ever knowing him. Ryan stood gawking at her in silence while once again perceptive to her red and distended eyes.

"I just want to know why you did it, Molly. I have to know why you *really* did it. I need the truth." "Come in, Ryan." She reluctantly made way for him to enter her home. "Just tell me, Molly, please." He cautiously and hesitantly entered while desperately beseeching her. "It's just that I can't believe you couldn't stand up to your father. I can't believe you would've given up so easily."

Molly moved closer to him while fidgeting nervously. "I didn't want to Ryan, that I swear to you, I didn't. I swear it on all that was good between us once, on all our promises to each other, and on my promise to you." The lump in her throat had reappeared without admonition, "If I could change what happened, or go back, I would, but you have to believe that I didn't want to." She gulped down with tremendous complexity, "You were my everything, Ryan. I loved you, *so* much." He placed his arms around her and held her confidently against him. He was overcome with a sense of belonging when he held her in his arms. It felt to him as though she was never gone when he realized that not much about her had change. Her hair still smelled exactly the way he remembered it, and the feel of her skin felt like nothing he had ever felt before or felt again since she's been gone. Molly felt safe, as though she had come home. In his arms was where she wanted to lay down her head, and never leave.

"Why didn't you tell me?" Ryan gently whispered, while tightening his hold over her. "I couldn't. My dad wouldn't let me. He thought that we were too young …" "Molly, I would never have turned my back on you, you *know* that. Your father knew that. You should've tried harder, Molly." He lifted her face just enough for their eyes to meet. "I don't know how I could have, Ryan. You weren't taking my calls …" Ryan let out a faint sigh, "I loved you. I've always loved you." He kissed her with fervor and urgency. She was without a doubt, the woman he fought to be alive for. He retreated slightly, and gazed into her eyes once again, "I was lost without you. There were days when I thought I could hear you call for me, but I couldn't find you. I could hardly breathe when I just thought about you, couldn't you feel it?" For the first time since Molly had returned, her heart had come alive again, and she by no means ever, had the desire to let Ryan go again.

"Ryan." He laid her down on the rug, and gradually undressed her. She laid in silence while sensitive to each fraction of her body quiver at his touch. She desperately desired from him to make her his one more time. He watched her as they made love, while Molly was overwhelmingly thankful that Ryan had absolved her. "I couldn't forget, Ryan. I couldn't. I came back for you." She devotedly whispered while attempting to find the kindness in his eyes that she once knew so well. Ryan kissed her through the tears that had begun to roll generously down his checks while he made love to her again. He craved the intimacy they once shared and was anxious to revive every little thing about them again, overwhelmingly obsessed with absorbing all about her as though for the first time. Ryan's heart was shattered as he recalled all that had gone wrong for them, but he didn't want the night to end. Molly held on to him as he swept her away to another time and a place she was once familiar with, reminding of what they once had.

When Ryan rolled onto his back, they both remained breathlessly silent on her living room floor, while staring impassively at the ceiling. Ryan unexpectedly leaped to his feet, and hurriedly clothed himself. He felt erratic culpability make its way into his heart and was unexpectedly convinced that he had made an enormous error in judgement. His mind persuaded him to retreat from her as fast as he could. He could not even once again, place his heart in jeopardy as he did before. His guilty thoughts turned to Flo, and he surprisingly felt blameworthy for what had just taken place with Molly. She intuitively knew that Ryan was remorseful for their impulsive behavior. "Ryan?" Molly was unpredictably frightened of what Ryan was feeling. "I shouldn't have come, Molly. I'm so sorry. I was caught up in, in another time, but it's a time long gone. It has run its course. You and me, that ship has sailed, Molly." He hoarsely tried to explain, powerless to look her in the eye. "Caught up in another time?" She made her way over to where he was standing. "Molly, I was caught up in yesterday. I am sorry. Flo's waiting for me, I'm with her now, and this was an enormous and unforgiveable mistake." He was desperate for Molly to understand that he wasn't geared up to step back into their past just yet. "How can you say that?" "Molly, listen to me, I carried on without you, I had to. I didn't know what else to do, and I couldn't let it control my life anymore, you know?" He paused briefly while frantic to find the words to express that nothing between them had changed.

"There was a time when I thought, I believed that I

Alice VL

couldn't go on, but I did. I started to forget." "But you said, you said you loved me, Ryan?" Ryan lowered his head in dishonor, uncertain of what to say next. "You said you loved me, Ryan!" He turned away from her while deliberately avoiding eye contact with her. "I needed closure, Molly. You were such a colossal part of my life once, and I realize now that my feelings for you are distorted. I loved you once, *then*. It's just not the same. I don't, I don't think I love you anymore, Molly. I just, I had to get closure, and now I have it. I'm sorry that things went too far tonight, I was caught up in a moment that passed a long time ago." Molly felt predictably humiliated by handing herself to Ryan on a silver platter and was once again aware of how polluted they had become. Ryan sensed that Molly was mortified, yet there was nothing he could say to her that he hadn't previously said. He turned away from her and shut the front door behind him as he hurriedly and urgently walked out. He had left her life for eternity, and the reconciliation she had so frantically hoped for; any likelihood that they might reunite, was crushed, and lost to her forever. She staggered over to the window that looked out over the ocean. Molly unwaveringly decided that Ryan Neves was no longer an element in her life, and that the time had come for her to put up the shutters of that chapter of her life, and stagger onwards, just as he had done. She was duty-bound to entirely disregard him, and stand up once more, without him. They were briefly caught up in the past. It was a meeting needed, but one they could never risk again.

Molly returned to her study and picked up the photograph of Ryan she arrogantly displayed on her desk. She made her way back downstairs to her closet, before she opened the carton box she had kept with countless of photographs and letters from their past, and callously flung the picture into the box. Molly jadedly and with tremendous disenchantment sat down at the end of her bed and wept feverishly. "It's over." She whispered, her voice trembling, "But, if it's all that I can have, Ryan, I'll love you in our past."

Ryan reached his apartment a few minutes later to find Flo anxiously awaiting him. "Where were you?" Flo was at once flustered when he nonchalantly strolled in. Ryan bowed his head and instinctively turned away from her, unsure of how to tell her the truth, but unwilling to lie to her. He was convinced that he could not accurately give her the details of what had taken place between him and Molly. "I went to see Molly." Flo felt panic grab at her heart, uncertain of what Ryan was about to say next. "I had to know, Flo. And, and it's made me realize that I want to be with you, not with Molly. When I saw her tonight, I knew it was over for us. What we had, must stay in the past. It belongs in the shadows of what I've left behind. My feelings for her have been tainted, but I needed answers from her. For me, it was more about getting closure from her. And now that I do, I am sure of one thing, it's you I want, if you'll have me?" He took Flo into his arms and held her doggedly against him. "I had this dream, this fantasy of having Molly back, but that's all that it was. It wasn't what I needed, this is, you and me." Flo held on to Ryan while desperate that that was all he had to say, but relieved and elated that he had chosen her over Molly. "I love you, Ryan." She lovingly kissed him as he hesitantly reciprocated, yet it was Molly's lips he unwittingly imagined touching his, and it terrified him. "Let's go to bed." Ryan smiled down at her, still feeling as though his world was fractured beyond repair. "I, I just have a few work things to finish. I won't be long." Flo was still grinning from ear to ear when she climbed into bed. Her heart convinced her that Ryan Neves belonged only with her.

Glumly, he sat down behind his hefty desk in his study where he struggled to busy himself with formalities that were waiting to be finalized before the next day. His mind relentlessly drifted back to Molly, and their love making played out over and over in his mind. Without any reservations, Ryan was definite that what had willingly and consensually taken place between them was an enormous blunder, but secretly, Ryan imagined that she had returned only to him, even if it was for only, one more moment in time. The distress he recognized in her eyes amplified almost by the minute, but he resolutely decided at that very instant that he would never lock himself into an inappropriate position as such again, and that Molly was a component of his past; a fraction that was beyond hesitation, a fixation from the past.

Alice VL

PATHS THAT COLLIDE

December 5th arrived far too abruptly for Molly. It was the day that she and Ryan shared their birthdays. Molly had published an additional two novels, but she lacked inspiration when it came to outlining her next one. Since that auspicious night almost two months ago, she had no grounds for enthusiastically moving onward, and noticed drearily that she had merely subsisted around all that were significant to her. All that she had hoped for and labored tirelessly for, had come crashing down on her, and she favored spending her days safely tucked away in her study while mindlessly gazing out over the ocean. When she did set foot outside her townhouse, she would promptly look in on Piper, but she rejected any and all further dinner invitations from Louis and Ida, out of fear of resentfully bumping into Ryan.

When she did agree to a quick visit with them, she would regularly listen in on Louis and Ida discuss Ryan and Flo, and it brutally disturbed her to learn that he had so easily and devotedly moved on with his new love as though their night together in no way influenced his decision of replacing her with

Molly

Flo.

Ryan had assembled a proper and unadulterated exertion with Flo. She blissfully accompanied him each time he dropped by Louis and Ida's home, cautiously afraid that he would scamper into Molly, but entirely mindful of the fact that he had no power over himself around her. Flo had grown increasingly unperturbed by Molly's affiliation with Ryan, and she convinced herself that it was a brand new and solid institution that they were embarking on. Ryan continued to think of Molly in secret and daily, but he was confident that he would reflect on her less, as soon as an ample amount of time had passed. He had recently begun hallucinating about her at night and would awake in terror while frantically and unsuccessfully reaching out for her. With misery engulfing and wholly overpowering him, Ryan would lie back down, and remind himself that she was lost to him for all eternity.

Molly was uncharacteristically short-tempered when she awoke earlier that morning, insufferably aware that her tears weren't awfully far off. When her phone unexpectedly rang, she was certain that it was Ida calling to wish her for her birthday. "Hello?" "Happy birthday, my friend!" Ida bellowed excitedly into the phone. "Thanks, Ida." "I haven't been able to really chat with you, come over for breakfast, please?" Molly could sense the fortitude in her voice. "Ryan isn't coming, I promise." Molly dawdled for an instant, "Alright." She had no intention of enduring misery on her birthday and wanted nothing more than to spend the morning with her close friend. While brushing her teeth curtly after she ended the call from Ida, Molly became unpredictably queasy, and was frenetic to recall whether she had eaten something off that might have upset her belly. She combed back her long blonde hair and fastened it droopily in her neck. She quickly glanced at her reflection in the mirror and was satisfied that she appeared better than she felt.

Alice VL

Molly

Ida had just placed her breakfast in front of her when she felt woozy yet again. Shortly after Louis had presented her with a cup of freshly brewed coffee, Molly was convinced that she would hurriedly have to make her way into the bathroom, and without wasting even a second. She sprinted down the passageway, offering no justification to either Louis or Ida who gawked at one other in bewilderment. "Let me go see if she's okay?" Ida bolted from her seat and set off to find Molly.

"Molly?" When Ida reached her, she was bending over the vanity. Ida was instantly worried when she realized that Molly had turned ashen. "I don't know? I've been feeling this way all morning, Ida." "Maybe you should go see a doctor?" Molly shook her head, "Let me just rinse my face, I'm sure I'll feel better." "Alright, I'll wait for you in the dining room." Molly stared at her manifestation in the mirror, oblivious of her sullen image staring back at her, while instantly reminded of another point in time that she felt as unsettled as she did that morning. "It can't be?" She whispered inaudibly while horror and apprehension made its way into her heart. When she lowered her head and glared into the hand basin, Molly was positive that it was a recurrence of what had taken place once before. What had transpired between her and Ryan that one forlorn and unforgiving night, was the one night that was about to revolutionize her life once again.

Alice VL

Molly

When she reluctantly ambled back into the dining room, she was instantly aware of Ryan and Flo's presence, brusquely after they had made themselves comfortable at the breakfast table. "Hi, Ida said you weren't coming?" She made an impressive effort to remain unruffled but was profoundly insightful to the fact that she felt as though someone was constricting her heart. "Oh, we're not staying. We were just passing by and decided to pop in quickly." Flo smiled at Ryan. Ryan glanced at Molly and noticed how frail she appeared to be.

"Happy birthday, Molly, we're getting old, huh?" Ryan got up and fleetingly kissed her on the cheek. "Thanks, you too Ryan. Listen, Ida …" She had only just managed to say her name before Flo uncouthly interrupted her. "You two share birthdays?" She was at once stunned that Molly and Ryan were born on the exact same day. "Yeah." Ryan let out a faint chuckle, "We were born on the same day in the same hospital. That's how our parents became friends." He gazed back over Molly, smiling when he thought back to all the birthdays they had celebrated together since. "Have a seat, Molly, finish your breakfast, it's getting cold." Louis signaled for her to take her seat before her breakfast was wasted.

Molly turned her attention back to her breakfast plate, and without prior notice or warning, became repelled yet again.

Alice VL

"I can't." She garbled before she ran down the passage one more time. "What's wrong with her?" Ryan was at once concerned by Molly's inexplicable conduct. Even though Ryan had reassured Flo that it was finally and eternally over between them, Flo could barely shake a nudging feeling that there were immeasurable fragmentary issues that had remained unresolved between them. He assured her that what had occurred between them was over and buried, yet he failed to declare or confess their one treacherous night together. He would persistently mention her when reflecting back on his childhood, leaving Flo painfully cognizant of the fact that Molly was an unforgettable and haunting element in Ryan's life while he was growing up. Flo was industriously unnerved by his reminiscence of his upbringing with Molly, but she was confident that Ryan's resentment of her would maintain the aloofness between them.

"I, I honestly don't know?" Ida hesitated, unsure of what to believe even though she was gaudily familiar with the warning signs. She was enormously perplexed and fanatically aware of the certainty that Molly had not at all engaged in a fervent relationship with another since her return, yet ignorant of Molly's one callous night with Ryan. Without thinking, Ryan leaped to his feet, and hastily made his way down the passage. He was mindful of the fact that Molly was of no concern to him any longer, but he could barely resist caring for, or tormenting about her. When he found Molly leaning into the hand basin, he instantaneously recognized how delicate and fragile she appeared to be all of a sudden, "Molly?" He took her hair into his hands, trying to keep her hair from dangling in her face.

"Ryan?" She felt terror well up inside her once again. "You okay?" Her heart had once again broken out into one gigantic shudder, afraid and unsure of what the next few days might hold. "Yeah, I don't know what's wrong with me?" She engaged in an extraordinary and heroic endeavor to shrug it off and pretend that she was in good health. She hurriedly rinsed her face, and turned to Ryan, gazing steadfastly into his eyes. With each breath of air she inhaled, she became increasingly desperate to tell him that she thought she was pregnant again. Molly was desperate to let him know that their one insignificant night together had given her a second chance, an opportunity to restore all that was broken and shattered, but when she gazed at him for just a moment longer, she was confident that no matter what she did right after all she had defaulted on, he would still never exonerate her, or feel about her as he once did.

"I must go." She almost pushed him out of her way, frantically attempting to pass him. She turned back to Ryan after wavering for a moment, but her mind furiously instructed her to keep going, and that there was no point in upsetting his life all over again. Ryan became increasingly anxious glaring at her, even though he reminded himself that she was no longer a notable aspect in his life. He had a sickening sensation that something was gravely and wide of the mark with her, and he was utterly astounded that he still felt the need to take care of her. He instantly wished that he would no longer feel as misplaced and immobilized around her. When Ryan reached the dining room, Ida was on the phone with Dr. McKenzie. They were all susceptible to the fact that Ida was scheduling a doctor's appointment for Molly. When she hung up, she handed Molly the particulars and turned back to face Ryan, "You should take her." She snapped accusingly and condemningly at him. He reluctantly glowered, gob smacked by Ida's behavior. "What did I do?" Ryan was confused, sure that he had stepped into an ulterior dimension. "No." Molly let out a faint giggle, "He really shouldn't." Ida turned, and hurriedly made her way back into the kitchen shortly after Molly left. They were all appreciative of the fact that there were no more uncomfortable and awkward silences.

When Molly caught a glimpse of her wristwatch while unwearyingly waiting in the reception area of the consulting rooms, she was disappointed that Dr. McKenzie was running late. Ida had insisted she schedule an appointment to see him earlier on, and when she arranged the meeting on her behalf, Molly knew that by hook or by crook, she had to keep the appointment to ensure that Ida had no grounds to harass her about it any further. Into the central part of Molly's being, she was positive that it would only be an affirmation of a pregnancy, she already knew to be factual.

"Ms. Starkey, please come through." The young assistant at the reception showed her into his consulting rooms. It all seemed so hauntingly familiar to her while she silently begged that in some way, it would all just be a horrendous nightmare or at the very least, nothing more than an upset tummy. After going through the memorable routine of blood pressure recordings and the submission of a sample of her urine, she took a seat directly across from Dr. McKenzie. Molly was devastatingly convinced of what he was about to tell her but was persistent in her faith that it might not be accurate. "I can't be sure, so I'd like to do a blood test. We should know without a doubt in a day or two." He hastily showed her to the bed, before a nurse approached her, and immediately drew her blood, leaving Molly feeling slightly shaken. "So, there's a chance that I'm not?" Dr. McKenzie instantly sensed the influential apprehension in her voice. "Well, there's always a chance, Ms. Starkey. I'll call you as soon as I have the results."

When Molly sauntered out of the consulting rooms, she

promptly made her way to a nearby coffee shop. She had just placed an order for a cup of coffee when she heard an identifiable voice behind her. "Molly?" She was stunned to find Ryan standing in front of her, "Ryan, what are you doing here?" She was snappishly out of place when he sat down beside her. "I had to collect a script for Flo from Dr. McKenzie, and on the spur of the moment, decided to stop for a quick coffee. You?" "I, I've just come from Dr. McKenzie." When the waitress brought their coffee, Molly was engulfed by a sickening feeling all over again. "Are you okay? It looks as though you've seen a ghost. Are you still not feeling well?" He swiftly shifted the coffee away from her when he realized that she had become unsettled by the mere whiff of the coffee in front of her. "No, I, listen Ryan, I have to run."

Before Ryan could intervene, Molly had speedily run out of the coffee shop. He was overcome by a niggling sensation once again that something was bitterly wrong with Molly, but he was drearily attentive of the certainty that Molly would not let him know if she was unwell.

He tensely dialed Ida's number and felt trepidation make its way into his heart. "Hey." "Hi Ryan, what's up?" "I just ran into Molly around the corner from Dr. McKenzie, do you know if anything's wrong?" Ryan hoped that Ida would tell him if she knew anything. "No, haven't spoken to her yet, why?" "She looks awful." Ryan was uneasily apprehensive. "Yeah, she's been like that for a couple of days now. I'll let you know if I know anything." When Ryan ended the call to Ida, he was convinced that Molly was ailing, but he was optimistic that it wasn't anything grave.

While driving home, Molly harshly interrogated herself as to what she would do if she were pregnant again. She questioned herself about whether she would let Ryan know, or if she should rather place a veil over it. Molly was certain that she would never have an abortion this time around, but she speculated on how she would successfully raise a child on her own, without Ryan. Molly reached her townhouse while still cavernously in thought. She became agonizingly aware of her tears that were bucketing down her cheeks. She was horrifically frightened, and utterly confident that there was in no way, a satisfactory or pleasant conclusion for her. She prayed while overcome with desperation that she was mistaken, but in the innermost part of her, Molly knew that she was pleading for much too much. "What am I going to do?"

She had just made her way into her study when she heard a thunderous knock on her front door. She tossed her handbag onto a sofa, and hastily made her way downstairs. "Ryan?" She was stunned to find him standing at her front door.

Alice VL

Molly

"I'm sorry I didn't call first, but we, you and I need to talk." He gently brushed past her as he made his way indoors. "What about?" Molly felt panic build up inside of her, while she guardedly closed the door behind him. "We can't go on like this, you and me, and Flo." Molly could sense that he was uncertain of what to say next. "I need to move on, Molly. So much has happened. You and I have changed so much and, we'll never, we can never be like we used to. I wanted to be the one to tell you, before you hear it from anyone else ..." He paused to take in what he hoped to be a bottomless breath. "Tell me what, Ryan?" Molly moved closer to him. "I'm going to ask Flo to marry me tonight."

He was anxious to find an indication in Molly's eyes to tell him that he was making a mistake, but Molly stared motionlessly at him, overcome with disbelief. It in no way at all, ever occurred to her that she would hear Ryan tell her that he wanted to spend the rest of his life with someone else, a woman who wasn't her. She not at all thought it possible that Ryan could love another woman, the way he once loved her. She stood inertly while listening to him make new-fangled plans with someone new, almost identical to the plans they once designed when they were just teenagers. She listened to him tell her that he had fallen intensely in love with Flo, and that he no longer wished to squander a moment more postponing their future together.

Alice VL

Molly

Molly was keenly responsive to her heart shattering yet again. The words that were reaching her ears slashed into her soul, and she gradually felt her tummy turn and her legs grow feeble. She walked up to him, and placed her hand on his chest, "Is that what your heart wants, Ryan? Is that what it takes to make you happy again?" Her eyes began to fill up with tears once again. Ryan gazed intently at her and was almost certain that he could visualize her heart being plucked out from inside her. He felt panic tug at his own heart, and it felt to him as though someone had taken his lungs into their hands and began squeezing at them. A flicker in her eyes beseeched him to come back to her, but the darkness in those same eyes confirmed a kind of suffering he never wanted to see in Molly's eyes again.

"All I do is hurt you, Molly. All I do is make you cry, and I can't see you like this. It breaks my heart. It does. I'm angry with you all the time. I'm so angry with you. At times, I want to take you into my arms, and hold onto you forever. I want to remember you and what we once had, but other times, I just want to hurt you so badly. I want to see you hurt. I want to see your pain, just as I am seeing it now. I just don't know how to be with you anymore." He despondently and unenthusiastically removed her hand from his chest. "When I stand in front of you like this, something tells me that we have to try again, that I have to try, that we must, but it also convinces me that we have become toxic together. There is something here between us that takes me back, and reminds me of what we once had, and I am terrified that I will never feel that way again. But I have learned that I don't *have* to feel like that again. I don't *have* to try and replace you; I just must move on." He paused, desperate to find an expression in her eyes to confirm to him that she disproves, "I will never forget what we had, Molly, and I guess I will spend a lot of time missing that, you, but anyway, what I'm trying to say is, it can never work between us now. Not after all that's happened. I trusted you once, and I had so much faith in you. It's not entirely your fault. I'm past blaming you. What we had was a lifetime ago, almost as though it all happened in another existence."

Ryan knew that he had to pluck up the courage and say the things he still wanted to say to her. "Molly, I've fallen in love with Florence, and I have to believe that we can make it work and be happy together. I *love* her. I honestly love her. What I feel for you is a connection to another life. A life we once lived but lost. I don't love you, Molly. I care, but I know that I don't love you, and I am sorry if what I am saying, hurts you. I want to settle down. I want to start a family, you know? Have kids and a house and a big yard. Now that I have my answers with you, I can finally put you behind me, and start again. Now that I am certain that I no longer love you, I can begin again. So, thank you for coming home, and showing me. It would have been the one thing I would have been stuck with, for the rest of my life. Can we just please forget about all that's happened between us, and stop hating each other so much? Can you forgive me for the way I treated you?" He affectionately took her hands into his. Molly bowed her head and made a distinct effort to gulp down on her tears. All she wanted to tell him was that she might be pregnant again. Molly wanted to beg him to wait, to linger for a moment and give her an opportunity to mend things with him just once more. Molly desperately wanted to plead with him to give her only one more chance to prove to him, to show him that he still loved her, but while the tears were rolling down her cheeks, she knew that Ryan Neves had given up on her a long time ago.

"I don't hate you, Ryan. I don't, but yes, I'm tired of all this guilt, the blame, everything. I am just tired of it all. You're right, we've both changed, and I had faith in you too. Maybe, we didn't love each other enough. I never gave up on you, but you gave up on me." Ryan stared at her, utter devastation in his heart, while Molly was gaudily aware of the tremor in his voice. "You don't believe that, do you Molly?" Ryan felt as though a dagger had pierced his heart. "Ryan, we were never meant to be. I *do* believe that now. Maybe, my dad knew more than what I gave him credit for. Maybe he saw what I couldn't or refused to see. Maybe, he saved us from a lifetime of bitterness." Molly was defeated. She had no further motivation to wrestle with Ryan.

Molly

Telling Ryan that she was horrified by the prospect of having a baby, one he had given her on a night they both shrugged off as a mistake, was no longer an option for her. Ryan was horrified by what she had just said, stunned that he felt so entirely conquered by her words.

She walked over to the front door, and opened it for Ryan, hoping that he would leave without another word, "I wish you both well, Ryan, I really do." "Thanks, Molly, honestly, thank you. I am truly sorry that our story had to end like this, even though you don't believe me and even if you think we were a mistake from the very beginning." Ryan walked out as swiftly as he had entered, as though he was never there.

When Molly could no longer see him, she viciously shut the door, and dropped to her knees. Living a life without Ryan was no life at all for her, and regardless of how much time had passed or how terrifically he despised her, she would never love anyone else again. It was always, only Ryan. It was all she knew. It was who she pined for since the day she was taken to the city. He was the man she had been waiting for her entire life, the man she had dreamed of night after night while alienated from, and the man she courageously tried to come home to. While Molly was on her knees crying for him, she angrily realized that she wished him all the best even though it meant letting him go.

Alice VL

Ryan drove away from Molly's townhouse, keenly perceptive to the notion that he would never recover from her, or effortlessly disregard what they once had. Each time their eyes met, he felt all the old feelings scuttle back, and it frightened Ryan to reluctantly acknowledge that it would forever only be Molly that owned the capability of instilling a feeling of immeasurable insecurity him, thereby leaving him uncertain of all that had ever meant a great deal to him. He convinced himself that he had to engage in a fearless and daring effort with Flo, it was a choice he had made, and a selection he wanted to see through to the very end. Ryan struggled to move past all the blunders that had taken place between him and Molly, and he persuaded his ego that an affiliation between two people should not at all be as wearisome as it had been with her and him. Ryan was satisfied that it was simpler and less daunting with Flo. He recognized how exhausting his approach to Molly was. He no longer intended to exert himself as rigidly as he once did with her, yet he was dismayed by the thought that they would never again be at a point where they once were.

The following morning, Molly awoke to an irrepressible urge to heave again. As she scattered into her bathroom, she unexpectedly heard Ida holler from the front door. After she swiftly doused her face, she unlocked her front door for Ida to enter. "Ida? Come in." "You look awful, Molly, did you go to the doctor?" "Yeah, they did blood tests and said they'd get back to me in a day or two." "So, listen, the reason I'm here so early is that Ryan and Flo are on their way over here." Molly was once again, staggered that Ryan couldn't simply leave her alone. "What? Why?" Molly was bewildered at once. "Ryan proposed to Flo last night, and she wants him to get the ring back, the one that he gave you." "Can't I just give it to you?" Ida nodded agreeably, "Well, that's why I'm here, so you're not alone. I know that you still love him, and I know it's hard for you." "I'm okay. Ryan came over last night and told me that he was going to ask her Ida, so, I know. I just don't want to deal with them. Can I take a shower while you wait for them?" Ida was at once despondent and nodded in agreement.

Molly hurriedly made her way to her bedroom, and quickly took the ring from her closet before she made her way back to Ida, "Here, just give it to them and ask them to leave. I can't face Ryan or Flo today. I don't want to." Molly promptly turned around and disappeared back into her bedroom.

When Ryan and Flo arrived brusquely afterwards at Molly's townhouse, Ida swiftly informed them that Molly was taking a shower. They all made their way to the front porch where Ida handed Ryan the ring. "She asked me to give it to you, she doesn't want to see you." Ida hesitantly turned to Flo. "I hope you guys are going to be happy together." She mumbled almost aggrievedly before unenthusiastically embracing Flo. Ryan was unexpectedly distressed by the notion that Molly no longer wanted to see him, and hurriedly made his way into her kitchen in an attempt to pour himself a glass of water, when her phone rang suddenly. Unconsciously, he answered the call, "Ryan Neves." He realized almost straight away that it was Molly's phone he had answered. "Good morning, Molly Starkey for Dr. McKenzie please." He was instantly aware of a hospitable voice at the other end of the call. When Ryan realized it was Dr. McKenzie calling for her, he was conquered by instant panic that had made its way into his entire being. He was once again certain that there was something acutely off-beam with Molly.

"She's not available at the moment, can I take a message?" Ryan was hopeful for more information. "Could you please ask her to call Dr. McKenzie, we'd just like to give her the results of her pregnancy test." Ryan stood as if frozen in time and instantly bowled over, while abruptly conscious of the fact that his heart was sharply racing. "Pregnancy test? Is she?" Ryan could barely resist questioning the outcome. "It's confidential, sir, please ask her to call us?" The voice on the other end was unyielding when she hung up at once. Ryan stood lifelessly with the receiver in his hand for what felt like forever, when he was instantly jolted back to reality as Ida and Flo made their way indoors. Ida knew by the look on Ryan's face that something had happened. He replaced the receiver and turned to Flo, "Listen, can Ida take you home, please? I have to speak to Molly. Her tests have just come back and, I just want to speak to her. Please don't ask questions. I'll explain everything later." "Is everything alright?" Flo walked up to Ryan. "I'm not sure? I just want to talk to her. I just have to find out from her, Flo." "Ryan, you're scaring me." Ida violently began tugging at Ryan's arm. "It'll be okay, Ida. Don't worry. I'll talk to you later, okay?" He reassured her before Ida and Flo grudgingly turned to leave.

Ryan had no hesitation in his mind that Molly was pregnant. He was positive that it had happened as a result of their one erroneous and regretful night together. He had to convey the message to Molly, and it terrified him to accurately visualize as to how she would respond to the news. Ryan surprisingly felt trepidation tug at his heart, but he convinced himself that they would deal with the news in a proper and appropriate manner, as they should have a long time ago.

Molly stood hopelessly in the shower for longer than was necessary, while pessimistically hoping that the water would magically rinse away all the torment and anguish that she was experiencing at that very instant. Hurt that by no means seemed to subside with time, and more often than not, Molly was persuaded that it could barely become any shoddier. When she finally climbed out of the shower, she was displeased to hear voices coming from her living room. "Shit, they're still here." Molly had just slipped on a pair of slacks and a sweater when she heard a slight knock on her bedroom door.

"Come in." She was under the flawed impression that it was Ida, there to tell her that Ryan and Flo had left. "Ryan? Didn't Ida give you the ring?" Molly was shaken to find Ryan walk through her bedroom door. "Yes, she did." He was at once vulnerable when he noticed her long hair hanging limply on her shoulders. "How are you feeling, Molly?" "Oh, I'm fine, really. I'm sure I was just worn out, the writing and well, things like that. Why are you in my bedroom, Ryan? Where is Flo? Where is Ida?"

"Have you heard from your doctor yet? Ida mentioned something about blood tests?" Molly could barely look him in the eye, and summarily turned away from him, unsure of how to respond without being dishonest. "I, yes." She hesitated. "And? Anything you want to tell me?" He was desperate to give Molly a fair chance to tell him the truth. "No no, I'm fine, Ryan. Really." She had a nagging feeling that there was something, by the way he was talking to her, that in no way seemed typical. Ryan stood

Alice VL

in calm while he glared at Molly and questioned whether she would have told him the truth about her condition had she taken the phone call earlier.

"Dr. McKenzie called while you were in the shower." Molly was instantly alarmed, while devotedly aware of the rage that had begun to build up inside of Ryan, even though he was making a courageous effort to be in command and control of himself. It was an emotion she was becoming accustomed to. Ryan was continuously infuriated with her, and despite how enormously she challenged to maintain her detachment from him, he constantly found a motive to remain irate with her. "You took the call?" She was predictably disturbed by what he was about to say next. "Yes, I did. Ida and Flo were on the porch when your phone rang, just hang on ..." When Ryan marched out of her bedroom, Molly sat down at the end of her bed as though in a daze. "Please, God, please don't let it be." Molly prayed staunchly and implored repeatedly while undeniably aware of her body that had begun to shudder. It became silent all of a sudden, leaving Molly distinctly relieved that they had all left. When she took the glass of water next to her bed, she virtually dropped it when she heard Ryan's voice behind her. "I've asked Ida to drive Flo home, we need to talk. I just wanted to make sure they had left, and they have." Ryan walked up to face her. By the expression on his face, Molly knew intuitively what he was about to say, and she understood that there was nothing she could say to him, that would alter what he already knew.

"Molly." He nervously sat down beside her on her bed, snickering despondently and nervously, "I suppose this time I'm the one to tell you, strange how things happen, isn't it?" Molly began to tremble feverishly; she could hardly hold onto her glass. Ryan took the glass from her and placed it on her dresser across from him. He gazed at her for a moment though endeavoring once more to find anything in her eyes to pledge to him that what he was about to tell her, would be what she sought to hear. After he initially hesitated, he faced her squarely in the eyes, "You're pregnant, Molly." He watched her intimately, and thoroughly scrutinized her, desperate to find a shimmer in her eyes that would validate her desire for this baby, a glimmer of hope as a guarantee that she would not reject their child as she did once before.

Molly closed her eyes in a distressed attempt to shut of the tears that were gushing liberally and unreservedly from her eyes. "How could they tell you?" Her hands were instantly frosted. "They didn't tell me, Molly, but by the way the nurse wouldn't deny it, I knew. All she said was that you need to call her for the results of your pregnancy test." He took her hands while keenly alert to how arctic she had become. "Would you have told me?" Ryan squeezed her hand. Molly turned to face at him, and for the first time since she left Harper Valley, she recognized the familiar, devoted, and adoring expression in his eyes. "I don't know. I mean, you just this very minute asked Flo to marry you?" She elected to remain truthful. The displeasure on Ryan's face was apparent when he got up and turned away from her. Ryan knew what the answer was, yet he had high hopes that it would be different this time around. His heart was crushed when he deliberated on all that she had hidden from him. He nervously questioned how she would have proceeded, had never taken the call. He irately accepted that Molly would never have told him, and it infuriated him. "I mean, Ryan, it doesn't mean that you're the baby's father." She inadequately orchestrated an unsuccessful defense for herself.

"Stop, Molly, just stop! Stop lying to me, just stop it! I don't know who you are anymore!" He paused as he frantically tried to recover his composure. "You can stand there and lie to me over and over again. You can try and hide this from me, but what I do know is, there is no-one else!" He was frenetic for her to understand that he remained closely acquainted with all the little details about her. Louis continued to tell him all there was to know. "Then why are you here, Ryan? Why do you keep punishing me over and over again? Why are you holding everything against me? I can't take it anymore! I made a mistake, and I am deeply remorseful for that, but for how long do I have to pay for it?" Molly rose to her feet at once, "I didn't plan for this to happen, Ryan. The baby, it was only one night! It happened only once! Who gets pregnant after just once?" She rambled on hysterically, "If I could change the whole lot, I would!"

"Change what? Molly, change what?" He grabbed her by her arm, instantly reminded of the abortion. "Ryan, you're hurting me." "Change what, Molly? Do you want to have another abortion?" He tightened his grip on her. "Ryan! You're hurting me!" Ryan let go of her arm before Molly disconsolately fell onto her bed. "No, Ryan, I can't go through that again. Not again." She began weeping ferociously. "You think that I wanted it. You keep blaming me for it. I can't stand this anymore!" Ryan sat down beside her and took her into his arms. He held her securely against him, permitting her to sob unreservedly. "Molly, we'll get through this, together. It happened again, and we can't change it. I'm sorry that it happened. The timing is just so wrong, but I'm here now, and I won't let you do this again, alone. But you have to promise me, Molly, you have to promise me that you won't do anything stupid. We just have to find a way to get along, for the baby's sake." He gently stroked her hair, desperate to reassure her that he would in no way at all, abandon her and their child. "What about Flo?" Molly gazed up at Ryan. "I'm going to be honest with her and tell her the truth, but that I still want her in my life, because I do. This doesn't change the way I feel about her, Molly." He paused to swab at a tear that had rolled down his cheek. "What happened between us that night, was a mistake, Molly. It should never have happened. But it has, and now, now we must make it work, with Flo. If you don't see fit, maybe she and I could take the baby and raise it?"

Molly freed herself from him, and turned away, unable to face him when her heart shattered into a million tiny pieces. Not only did Ryan substitute her with Flo, but he intended to take her child away from her and give it to her to mother. "Do you love her that much, Ryan?" Ryan lowered his head, and even though he diffidently believed he did, his answer remained unchanged, "Yes, Molly, and I want a chance with her." Molly smiled sorrowfully when she detected the authenticity in Ryan's eyes. She felt her heart rupture once more while convinced that she had destroyed any possibility of a life together.

"I didn't realize how much, how much you love her. I want you to have that chance with her, and the baby, I don't know how I feel about it. I just don't want to decide today." Ryan clasped her hand before he kissed her tenderly on her cheek and walked away from her. Molly sobbed despondently into her pillow when she heard the front door close behind him.

Alice VL

When Ryan embarked on his drive back home, he continuously relived their one night of treachery together. Ryan was consumed with remorse over what had taken place between them and was wholeheartedly conscious to the nagging reality of having to tell Flo that Molly was going to have a baby, his child. When he turned into his driveway, he parked his car and switched off the ignition. He sat silently while staring out ahead of him, unsure of how to confess to Flo about his infidelity.

When he entered their home, he found Flo sitting out on the terrace. He shoved his car keys into a drawer, and hurriedly walked out to meet her. "Hello handsome!" She got up to greet him but at once noticed how red Ryan's eyes were. She was conspicuously aware of the tears that were about to roll from them. "Ryan?" She took his face in her hands. Ryan turned away from her, defenseless and powerless to find the words to tell her of his unfaithfulness. "Is it Molly? What happened?" "Flo, sit down, please." He took an empty chair and placed it directly across from her.

When Flo sat down, Ryan cautiously sat down in front of her. He lowered his head and clutched her hands in his. Flo felt terror replace the panic she had been aware of earlier and was fearfully anxious of what he was about to disclose. "Ryan?" Ryan gazed into her eyes and was agonizingly aware of how frightened Flo had suddenly become.

"Florence, I have to tell you something, and I wish to God I didn't have to. I would give almost anything not to have to tell you this." He began explaining, while tightening his grip on Flo's hands. Flo glowered again, overwhelmed by the burning sensation that what he was about to tell her, was not at all anything she wanted to hear. "Alright?" "That night, that night I went to see Molly, do you remember?" Flo nodded suspiciously. Ryan lowered his head again, struggling to find the words that were not at all reaching his mouth. "It just happened, Flo. I knew straight away that it was a mistake and I wish, I wish I could take it back, but it just happened."

Flo glared questioningly at him before she understood unerringly what he was telling her. "You slept, you slept with Molly? That night?" Flo was frantic to discover the truth and felt her own tears shimmer in her eyes. Ryan's tears had begun to flow without stinting from his eyes, and once again, he bowed his head in shame and more importantly, in remorse. "Ryan!" Flo leaped from her seat while Ryan remained silent. Flo was abruptly horrified by what he had done. "Look at me Ryan!" Ryan got up to face her. "I chose you, Flo, and I told Molly that. I asked you to marry me last night, because I *do*. I do want to marry you, and I do want to spend the rest of my life with you. I *do*. I knew it that night, I just don't know why or how it happened?" Flo hunched as her legs gave way beneath her before she broke into rigorous tears once again. Ryan took her into his arms and held her forcefully against him. "Do you love me, Ryan?" Ryan was excruciatingly aware of the fact that her world that had begun crumbling around her. He pulled her closer to him, "I do, I love you, Flo." She turned away from him and made her way back to her chair. She sat down slowly and pulled her knees up to her chin. "Why are you telling me, Ryan? Why *now*?" Flo whispered, certain that there was more to their one night of deceit than what Ryan was telling her.

He once again took the seat in front of her, gulping back on his tears. "She's pregnant, Flo." Flo burst out into tears yet again before he took her into his arms and allowed her to sob liberally. "I don't want to live without you, Flo. I want to make this work with you, but I can't, I can't agree to an abortion. I can't ask her to, and I can't let her." He bravely tried to explain how tremendously harrowing the entire state of affairs was. "No, you can't Ryan." She agreed wretchedly. "What do I do?" Flo turned away from him and recognized the fact that even though he was the father of Molly's child, she wholly adored him, and the thought of losing him terrified her almost to death. "We'll deal with it. You and I, we'll find a way, if that's what you want?" Ryan

Molly

kissed her, overcome by sadness, but desperate for a way out with Flo by his side. "More than anything, Flo."

Alice VL

GOING AROUND IN CIRCLES

Without prior announcement or caution, Christmas had crept up on Molly unexpectedly. On Christmas Eve, she agreed to spend the holidays with Ida, Louis and Piper. She was undoubtedly happiest when she spent moments with them, and for the first time in what felt like an eternity, Molly was more at home and calmly at ease with her life as it was. She more frequently longed for her parents and was thrilled to find that as time had passed her by, she gleefully found exculpation and absolution for her father make its way into her heart. Even though Flo had remained wounded and incensed by Ryan and Molly's betrayal, she was geared up to accept Ryan in any form that he presented himself as.

When Flo and Molly once thrashed out that, that had taken place between her and Ryan, Molly swore to her that it would in never happen again, and she reassured her that she was repentant for her role in their treachery. She gave Flo her word that she would maintain a suitable remoteness from Ryan, and even though Molly guaranteed Flo that it was over between them long before she had returned, Flo had a nudging feeling that it would in no way really be over between them. She reluctantly witnessed the manner in which Ryan would withdraw from her at times, and it constantly reminded her of the love he once had for Molly.

She would overhear him ask Louis how Molly was doing, and all it had established for her, was a confirmation of certainty that he barely felt the same way about Flo, as he once did about Molly. Flo was zealously aware of the way he gazed at Molly when he thought nobody was watching. Flo hungered after that brand of fondness from Ryan, but she accepted in the innermost part of her, that Molly had claimed his heart long before she ever showed up in his life.

Although Flo's revulsion and antagonism was impossible to disregard, Molly was confident that when enough time had gone by, she would have no alternative but to pardon them, and enthusiastically build a new life together with Ryan. Ryan struggled to restore confidence in her, and effectively persuade her of his love for her, but she never truthfully believed him. He was desperate to demonstrate his adoration for her on numerous occasions, yet Flo found his betrayal with Molly utterly and irreversibly despicable.

"You slept with her!" Flo would shout out after yet another heated squabble about Molly. Ryan would bow his head, disgraced by his actions, and with no indication of what to say to her. "I'm sorry, Flo, it shouldn't have happened." He would repeatedly illuminate over and over, but with each argument, there was an increase in hostility. He was convinced that she would never or at all, ever have the confidence in him, she once had.

"Why, Ryan, why? Just tell me why?" Flo would press him for answers, knowing there had to be more to it simple being a mistake. "I don't know? It just happened. I was caught up in the past. It just happened, Flo." "Yes, and now there is a child!" Flo would snap abruptly. "It should never have happened, Flo. It would be so much more straightforward without the baby." Mostly, Flo would feel mercy for him, but she could barely contain her resentment towards both Ryan and Molly every once in a while.

Molly sat quietly at her desk, nervously clutching the phone in her hand for what felt like hours. She hesitated over and over again, before she slowly dialed the number, she wasn't sure would still exist. When she heard her father's familiar voice, her heart began to thump wildly. "Dad?" Molly hoarsely whispered while instantly apprehensive of his response. "Molly? Baby girl?" Molly could at once ascertain the disbelief and astonishment in her father's voice. "Daddy." She was aware of an unexpected shudder in her voice. "How are you, honey? Where are you? Molly? I am so sorry, my girl. If I could go back and change …" "Dad, stop! It's alright, daddy, I'm not upset anymore." She presented her father with the absolution he so urgently desired. "I love you so much, my girl. If only I had listened to you." Molly swallowed back on the ever-familiar restricting lump in her throat. "How's mom?" "She misses you, angel." He swiftly handed the phone to Sue. "Molly?" "Oh mommy!" Molly suddenly broke out into tears and wept inconsolably into the phone. "Where are you?" "I'm home mom, and I'm fine, don't worry about me. I've published five novels in just as many years." "Yes, I know honey, I've read them all and I am so proud of you, my baby girl." Molly was thankful that they had not forgotten her. "How are Tyron and Megan?" "Oh, they're doing wonderfully. Tyron has just received his high school diploma, and Megan will finish school next year. They ask about you all the time." Sue continued to give her a run-down of the life she had left behind. "When can we see you, Molly?" "Soon, mom, I promise." "Can I talk to dad again please, mom?" Molly smiled when she heard her father's voice again. "Hey baby …" "Daddy, I love you, I truly, truly love you. I just wanted, I just wanted you to know that. I also want you to know that, I understand, daddy. I'm so sorry for what I said to you the day I left. I never, ever meant it daddy because, I just love you so much." "Oh, Molly honey, it wasn't your fault. I was terrible to you." "Please tell me you found Ryan?" He was frantic to know that he hadn't entirely destroyed his daughter's life.

"I see him daddy, but he, he just doesn't love me anymore." James felt his heart being ripped from his body, and he was once again aware of the brutal suffering he had inflicted on his daughter. "It's not your fault, daddy. I love you, and I'll call again. Merry Christmas, Daddy." Even though she yearned for her family, Molly was proud of herself for taking the first step towards reconciling with her parents, but she wasn't quite prepared to let them know about the baby.

Alice VL

Molly

On Christmas morning, Molly was contented with her decision of reaching out to her parents, and ecstatically made her way up the path of Ida's home. She was instantly apprehensive when she noticed Ryan's car parked in the driveway. "Oh no." Piper ran up to meet her, before Molly handed her a Christmas gift. "Hello, and Merry Christmas." Molly greeted the entire gang when she reluctantly entered their home. Ryan got up to kiss her on the cheek, leaving Molly feeling awkward when she could sense that Flo had not yet absolutely excused her for her duplicity. She was convinced once again that Flo could barely tolerate seeing Ryan act in a friendly or civil manner towards her. "How are you feeling?" Flo instantly bolted to her feet mumbling inaudibly which in turn, caused Molly to realize that spending Christmas together was a mistake. Even though she didn't anticipate that Ryan and Flo would be joining in for the Christmas celebrations, she resolved to rather spend the day at home, alone.

"Ida, it's really uncomfortable, and I would rather not have come if I had known they were going to be here." "Now you listen to me, Molly, you're my friend, and Flo knows that. If this is how she's going to be, *she* can leave." Ida glared accusingly at Ryan. He got up in an attempt to search for Flo, who had promptly excused herself, "Merry Christmas you guys, we have to get going." Flo turned back to Ryan when they walked back in.

Alice VL

Molly

"Are you coming?" "No, actually, I'm going to stay. You are being childish, Flo." Ryan had no intention of leaving anytime soon, and for some inexplicable reason, he yearned to be around Molly for just a little while longer. Ryan was abundantly aware of the fact that he should not at all feel the way he felt around her, but he was powerless to persuade himself to leave with Flo. When Flo stormed out, Molly felt responsible for her sorrow. She knew that her presence inflicted enormous discomfort for her, and she conceded to the fact that it was never Flo's fault. She and Ryan alone were to blame for their indiscretion, not Flo. Molly ran out directly after her and caught up with Flo just as she had climbed into her car, "Flo, please stay, please." Molly pleaded with her. "I have to be somewhere else anyway and was just leaving." Flo glared at Molly, her tears shallow in her eyes. "Just let him go, Molly." Molly watched her closely and was convinced that she could almost visualize Flo's broken heart. "I am trying ..." "Why don't you just have another abortion? It will be better for all of us. Ryan loves me now Molly, and the baby, the baby will just make matters worse. I don't want to be that baby's mother. I don't want to raise that baby! I can't, Molly, I don't want to. How am I supposed to look into that child's face every single day, and be reminded of the betrayal, of the love Ryan once had for you. I want Ryan to be the father of *my* babies, ours." She climbed out of her car to face Molly. Molly stared at her incredulously, "Is that

Alice VL

what Ryan wants?" Flo remained silent for a while before finally gazing back at Molly. "He wants it to work, Molly, between us and he has said so many times that it would have been so much easier if you weren't pregnant. I really don't know what he wants, why don't *you* ask him? Maybe he'll tell you, because he isn't telling me a damn thing!" She furiously turned away, and overwhelmed by emotion, she marched back into Ida's house. Molly noticed how utterly distraught Flo was and at that very moment, and she knew without a doubt that there was only one thing left for her to do. She was answerable for the aloofness between Ryan and Flo, and by any means necessary, she had to try to give Ryan his life back. She had to make way for Ryan and Flo to have an authentic chance of an unadulterated life together. For the very first time since she discovered her pregnancy, Molly realized that she was holding them back and because of that, she was unwittingly keeping them trapped in limbo. Molly finally understood her father and why he made her abort her child. She loved Ryan more than she loved her child, and the time had come for Molly to do the right thing for once in her life. She had to retreat, and willfully surrender while discreetly escaping Ryan's life.

She was indebted to him for allowing her to be such an enormous part of his life for as long as she had been, but she was excruciatingly aware of the fact that things would never be the same for them, despite the fact that they were having a child together. It no longer concerned her that it was tremendously thorny for her, she was obligated to recognize that it was long over between them, and she was forced to free herself from her dream of being Ryan's girl once more. She knew she would never recover from losing Ryan, and she would be able to discard all the years they shared together, but she couldn't pardon herself for what she had done once before, and for what she was about to do.

Molly walked back inside just a few minutes after Flo and said a hurried goodbye to her friends. When she reached the door, she turned back to Ryan, "Ryan, I just, I am saying goodbye to you, at least, until the baby comes. I want you to be happy, and I want you to have a great life with Flo. She is great, and the two of you are wonderful together. I am so sorry for all that I have done, and all that I am still liable for. I never meant for things to turn out like this, and all I can ask from you is to forgive me. Maybe one day, what I'm trying to say is, I am so thankful to have had you in my life, and I will never ever forget all that you meant to me." Molly discovered that the bulge in her throat had grown larger as she struggled to find the words to tell Ryan how undeniably invaluable, he was to her; instead she summarily walked out the door.

Alice VL

Ryan was anxious as he listened to what she was saying. Something inside him whispered that he would never see her again. Ida was undoubtedly unhappy that she left, and the glares she exchanged with Flo made it apparent to Ryan and Louis that she would ideally have spent the holiday with Molly. When Molly glanced back at Ryan, she prayed that he would finally be at peace, and that he would desist from being so incredibly irate and angry with her. It was a small penalty to forfeit, to be able to one day witness Ryan in high spirits again, and when she peered at him one last time, Molly was certain that Ryan and Flo would find tremendous bliss with one another. Flo was a pure and considerate woman with a gigantic heart.

She adored Ryan, and it thrilled her at no end to accept that he would be loved and cared for. She was fed-up with her declaration that they were in combat with one another, and she knew that she had to put an end to all their issues for once and for all. The compulsion rested squarely on her shoulders to enforce the essential and crucial changes, and even though they would perhaps one by one discard her, she was confident that Ryan would one day understand, just as she understood why her father had compelled her once before. She muttered a swift goodbye to all and headed home as if in a daze. Ryan had an unexpected urge to run after her, but when he noticed the despair and discouragement in Flo's eyes, he reluctantly let Molly go.

Molly headed almost as though in a straight line for her desk when she reached her home, and promptly paged through their local telephone directory while she began to quiver almost at once. She speedily found the number she was searching for, and nervously dialed it. "Marie Stopes, good day?" She was relieved to hear a forthcoming voice on the other side. "Hello?" Her heart demanded that she linger and wait, to be patient for just a little while longer, but her mind instructed her to go ahead, there was no possibility of an acceptable outcome and at the same time, she owed it to herself to shield her heart from Ryan Neves. "Hi, my name is Molly Starkey. I'd like to make, I'd like to make an appointment for, for …" Molly scuffled with her words. "It's all right, dear. How far along are you?" "I'm, a little, a little over two months, actually, closer to three." "No problem then, we've just had a cancellation and I can squeeze you in at first light. Does that suit you?" "That's fine, thank you."

The appointment was scheduled and confirmed for just after seven the following morning, and even though Molly felt that she could hardly breathe, it made no different to her how immoral it was for her to go ahead. She had survived it once before, and she was positive she could bear it one more time. Ryan had no trouble despising her. She was convinced that he

Molly

could not loathe her any more than he already did.

Alice VL

Molly

Molly awoke early the next morning, and after a rushed shower, she heard a faint knock on her front door. When she glanced at the clock against the wall, she was surprised to realize that it was just after six, entirely aware of the fact that sun hadn't risen yet. Before she made her way down the passage, Molly hastily placed a towel around her wet hair, and quickly covered herself with an evening robe. "Flo?" She was utterly astounded and bowled over to find her standing there. "Hey Molly, how are you? I was on my way to, I just needed to stop by …" "I'm fine, thanks for asking, I think?" Molly was limply ignorant as to why Flo had pitched up on her doorstep. "About yesterday …" "Oh, it's alright, Flo, please don't worry about it anymore." "No, Molly, you don't understand." Flo stumbled over her words. "It's just, I love him. I just want you to understand that I am not a mean person. I am not horrible by nature, I just love him so much, and I am so scared of losing him to you and to the baby." Molly walked up to Flo and placed a gentle hand on her shoulder. "It's over between us, Flo, and what happened, the baby, it should never have happened. Ryan loves you; he adores you, and he wants a chance with you. I know that. He made it clear that he was desperate for a chance to make things work with you. Undeniably, it was hard for me in the beginning, but I understand now. It's you he wants; how can you not know that? Everything is going to work out just fine, you'll see. Even though you have no reason whatsoever, just trust me, okay?" Flo unexpectedly flung her arms around her, "Thank you, Molly." She embraced her snugly, "Darn, my cell phone battery is flat, could I use your phone?" "Yeah, sure. It's upstairs in the study. I'm just going to change or else I'm going to be late for, a get-together." Flo swiftly made her way upstairs, and hurriedly dialed a number using the landline on Molly's desk. The phone had just begun to ring when Flo's eyes caught a memo scribbled on a sheet of paper. She unconsciously replaced the receiver down, and secretly picked up and read the note. "07h00 – Marie Stopes".

Flo was familiar with the medical center and was ardently aware that it was the only legal abortion clinic in the country. She was bleakly alert to what Molly was preparing to do. She sat in horror for a moment, all the while attempting to sway herself away from the note and overlook the reality of seeing the scrawling on that little pad. She knew that Ryan would never forgive Molly for massacring his child once again, and she slyly knew that it would be the answer to all her prayers. It would allow her and Ryan a fair possibility of a fresh start and a brand-new beginning, and perhaps someday, she would be the one to bear his children. She gazed out over the ocean while still holding the note in her hand with calamitous ambiguity. She tried to find added reasons to keep up the ignorance and remain quiet while allowing Molly to go forward with the abortion, but the longer

Molly

Flo weighed out the pros and the cons, the more her mind incessantly prompted her that she was better than that. As much as she adored Ryan, as insecure and uncertain as Molly had made her feel, she could not sit by, and watch Molly make the exact same mistake for a second time. With misery in her heart, Flo sorrowfully recognized and forlornly accepted that she wouldn't have the capability of replacing Molly in Ryan's heart.

Her heart was aching, but she grudgingly commanded herself to do what was respectable for both Molly and Ryan. She hastily made her way downstairs where she bumped into Molly on her way out. "Did you come right?" Flo could barely look her in the eye, and spontaneously excused herself. "Thanks, Molly, I did, thanks." As Flo was about to close the front door behind her, she turned back to Molly. "You said you have an appointment. Today? It's the day after Christmas?" "Oh, that, yes, just some friends." "Okay then, bye!" Flo yanked her phone from her purse and without wasting a second, she dialed Ryan's number,

"Hey." She was at once breathless when she realized that her batter was about to die, but that she just had to tell Ryan. "Hey, my battery is about to die. Where are you?" "At the office, just sending a few emails. Why, what's the matter?" Ryan at once sensed the urgency in her voice. Flo hesitated for a moment, "I'm not sure but, it's Molly. I must be crazy to tell you this, and I could be wrong …" Ryan at once felt his heart miss a beat. "What's wrong with Molly?" His heart had begun to thump as though it was about to leap out of his chest, "Flo, what's the matter?" "I've just come from her place. I went up to her study to make a phone call, and I saw a note." Ryan remained silent while waiting for her to make her point. "I think, I think she's having an abortion this morning, and it's all my fault, Ryan. I told her that it would be easier for all of us, and that the baby just got in the way." Ryan was at once flustered. His heart was pounding as though bouncing around inside of him. "What? Where?" "Marie Stopes, I think." "What did you say to her, Flo? What did you say to her? You better pray that she doesn't do it, Flo, so help me." Ryan grabbed his car keys, and apprehensively ran out of his office. Flo began to snivel, and when she tried to respond to Ryan's questions, she was tearfully aware that he had hung up. Ryan frantically reached his car but was devastatingly conscious of the fact that he was almost thirty minutes away from the medical center. He prayed that he would make it in time to stop Molly from making the second biggest mistake of her life. His heart was twigging at the thought of her going through another termination, and he felt colossal resentment towards Flo.

Molly glanced at the clock and realized that she had twenty minutes to spare before her appointment. She had to leave straight away if she was to be on time. She snatched her

Alice VL

purse and car keys in one motion, before she ran out to her car. While driving to Marie Stopes, Molly was astounded by how composed and unruffled she was. She felt no sentiment at all, and when she turned her thoughts to Ryan, Molly was satisfied that he could in never again wound her as rigorously as he already had. He would never forgive her, and there was nothing more left for him to come back to. Their baby would have held him in reserve for years to come, but she was not at all geared up for the hurt and antagonism that came along with it. She was desperate to press forward without Ryan, while destroying all evidence of their life together and the love they once shared. It was the only way she knew how to.

When she walked up the pathway of the medical center, Molly hurriedly switched off her mobile phone, and tossed it into her purse. She took a deep breath, and effortlessly opened the enormous glass doors before she made her way to the reception area. "Hi there." "Hi, I'm Molly, Molly Starkey?" She hesitated for an instant. "Yes, here you are. Take a seat, and we'll attend to you shortly." Molly tensely sat down in an empty seat and was appreciative of the fact that she was the first patient of the day, which left her feeling distinctly tranquil. It all felt overwhelmingly proverbial to her and ignited a multitude of agonizing memories. Molly felt a tear roll down her cheek, and summarily wiped it away, frightened that someone might discover her hesitation.

Molly

When she thought about Ryan again, her hands began to shudder slightly, while the restricting lump in her throat mercilessly and without warning returned. Molly was anxious to settle on how she would tell Ryan, Ida and Louis that she had once again executed her child, but at that distinct moment, not much else mattered to her other than getting through that day. Molly had to press on if she wanted to move forward with her life, and act as though Ryan Neves was in no way a part of her very survival.

Ryan raced through the streets of Murray Field as expressly as was safely possible, while incessantly dialing Molly on her mobile phone, even though he continuously reached her voice mail. He could think of nothing more than reaching her in time, but was deathly fearful that he in fact, may already be too late. He was unexpectedly and abruptly plunged into the realization that he was frenetically striving to salvage them so much more, than only seeking to liberate their child. For the first time since Molly had returned, all Ryan could reflect on was how he so urgently wanted to bring her back to him. He could think of nothing more than how unrelenting his love for her was through all that had gone wrong between them, and how unreservedly discontented and hopeless he was without her. Ryan's only mission on that day, the day after Christmas, was to rescue Molly from herself.

Alice VL

Molly

"Come through, please Ms. Starkey." Molly nervously stood up from the seat and straightened her coat, irrefutably conscious of the fact she was surprisingly composed. "Dr. Davis would like to have a word with you before we start. Its standard procedure, so don't worry." She showed Molly into his office. "Good morning." His voice was calm and unruffled, leaving Molly feeling strangely at ease straight away. "Sit down." He showed her to an empty seat. "I have to ask if you are sure about this. We've had so many patients in the past that act on impulse, and they never really recover from it." Without warning, Molly was immensely fearful, and was certain that Dr. Davis had sensed her apprehension. "I'm sure, doctor, it's not the first time." "You know Ms. Starkey, for whatever reason you are doing this, you have to be entirely sure that you are doing this for the right reasons?" Molly understood what he was trying to say, but she had made a decision, and she was determined to see it through until the bitter end. "I'm sure, can we just do it, please?" "Alright then, come through please." He led the way into an adjacent room. Molly changed into a hospital robe and made her way to a bed in the corner of the surgery. She swiftly glanced around her, and the familiarity of it all was hauntingly reminiscent of a moment, once before. She began to sob silently, confident that she was no different or superior to her father. She alone was accountable for her actions at that very instant. She cautiously

Alice VL

climbed onto the bed, and calmly laid down before taking in a deep breath. Molly closed her eyes, and unwittingly thought of Ryan. She struggled with all her valor to recall the lighthearted and blithe boy from Harper Valley, but all she could identify with, was the disgust and repugnance in the eyes of the man from Murray Field. He was no longer her Ryan. He was no longer the Ryan she adored and cherished. The one she would catch affectionately and amorously gazing at her. There were no traces of the boy she once knew so well. She had left him behind a long time ago, and she was convinced that she would never again, find him in another time.

An older nurse speedily approached her while she was still deep in thought. With a needle in her hand, she fiercely began hunting for a perceptible vein in her arm. "My name is Nurse Julie. This won't hurt at all, little miss." She wrestled incessantly with her arm, while trying to find an exposed vein, and by how cold Molly's hands had become, she recognized that her blood pressure had begun to plummet. "Are you okay?" Nurse Julie promptly paused to check on Molly. "Fine, just nervous." Dr. Davis entered and made his way around to Nurse Julie when he noticed that she was irritably trying to locate a vein. "What's wrong, Julie?" "I don't know? I can't seem to find a vein?" He took Molly's arm and patted it gently, "There we go." He retreated just a tad, allowing Nurse Julie to administer the general anesthetic. Molly was jolted by a sudden panic that had unexpectedly and without caution entered her body. She gaped at the needle in repulsion and was horrifically aware of the enormous and mortal mistake she was about to make. "No, wait!" Molly cuffed the needle from her arm just as Nurse Julie had begun to introduce the numbing sedative. "I can't do this. I can't do this again." She sat straight up on the bed, glancing incredulously at Dr. Davis. "I am sorry, Dr. Davis. I'm really sorry, but I can't do this. You were right earlier." Molly leaped off the bed and disappeared into the adjoining office where she had kept her clothes. "I just can't do this." Molly was in no doubt when she hurriedly dressed into her own clothes.

When Ryan frantically pulled up in front of Marie Stopes, he at once noticed her car in the parking lot and prayed that he wasn't too late. He rushed through the gigantic class doors, desperate to find her as soon as possible. "Where is she?" Molly was stunned to hear his familiar voice within spitting distance from her. "Molly Starkey, where is she?" Molly's heart was racing at a tremulous speed, profoundly conscious of the fact that she could barely breathe. "Ryan?" She nervously peered around the corner. "Molly!" He pressed past the nursing staff, and hurriedly made his way towards her. She was defeated with trepidation when she noticed Ryan approach her, and the expression on his face was one that Molly resolved to never, ever witness again.

Alice VL

Molly

"Am I too late? Please tell me that I'm not too late!" He grabbed a hold of her arms while pleading with his eyes. "How did you know?" Molly was shaken and stunned to find him there. "Just tell me you didn't?" He persisted without delay, "Molly, please, don't do this to me again." "Ryan, let it go, what's done is done. It's over now." Molly freed herself from Ryan before he instantly clutched her hand into his, "I'm begging you, Molly." "How did you know, Ryan? Why did you come here?" Molly was unexpectedly annoyed. "Flo, she told me." "Flo? How did she know?" "She said that she saw a note in your study. At first, she didn't want to say anything, but …" He began choking on his words before Molly furiously interrupted him. "I, I can't deal with you right now, Ryan. Just go home. Go home to Flo." Molly bellowed angrily and dashed out through the glass doors of the medical center. Ryan caught up with her just seconds before she reached her car. It had started to rain aggressively, but they were both oblivious to the fact that it had come crashing down on them in full force. "Molly, wait!" Ryan grabbed her arm once again. "Why did you do this? I wasn't there for you the last time, but I'm here *now*. I told you that I'd never leave you, Molly, please. I know that you didn't want to do it the first time. Why did you to it now, again? We could've made it work." He was desperate for an explanation while horrendously certain that his heart had been shredded into a million infinitesimal pieces. "I can't do this, Ryan, I just can't do this with you anymore." She irately swabbed the pestering and irrepressible tears from her cheeks. "We could've made it work, Molly. I don't understand? What did Flo say to you?"

Molly placed her purse in her car, and pessimistically turned back to face him. She was grimly reminded of all the anguish and resentment that had been living inside of her for all the years gone by. Anger for not standing up to her father, fury for not shielding her baby, and rage for being rejected and discarded by Ryan. She began hammering at him violently after she gave herself permission to weep unreservedly. For far too long, she had reluctantly gulped down on her tears, and veiled her sorrow from the world. For too long had she had stood courageously in front of Ryan, leaving him to thrash her incessantly. Molly allowed herself to fall apart after she could no longer console her wounded and injured heart. "What do you want from me, Ryan? I came *back*. I came home, but you were the one that was gone. I didn't get myself pregnant, Ryan. When I see you and Flo, don't you know that I can't do this anymore! I'd rather you hate me than be a part of your and Flo's life." Ryan stood motionlessly, and he swore he could hear her the shattering sounds of her heart. "I am nothing to you anymore, nothing! You never let a chance go by without reminding me, without making me feel like I'm the worst person alive. You can't just leave me to carry on with my life. No! You'll never be happy until you break me, and I just don't know how to make things right with you anymore. Why can't you see how much I still love you?" She recklessly buckled into his arms while continuously pounding at him. Molly sobbed feverishly in his arms, convinced that she would by no means ever, be capable of voluntarily stopping her tears. Her core was gradually, but progressively surrendering to a torturous and undignified demise when she persuaded herself that Ryan would never understand how profoundly she needed him to survive, and how acutely she loved him.

"I know that you want to try with Flo, and I am fully aware that the baby will just make things so much harder, but while I was laying there, I, I just couldn't do it again, Ryan, I couldn't, and that's alright, because I can do this without you. I *can* do this. My heart won't let me give my baby up. You can carry on, pretend it never happened. I can do this." Ryan could barely absorb all she was saying as her tears continued to flood her face. All he distinctly heard was that she failed to go through with the termination. He closed his eyes, and said an inaudible prayer while thanking God for stepping in. Ryan held her forcefully against him, and at that very moment, he understood that he had enormously messed up his relationship with Molly. Ryan was abundantly clear of the fact that James was not the only one answerable for wounding Molly, he too, had participated in the enormity of her injuries.

The revelation that he had turned his back on Molly when she needed him the most became almost too distressing for Ryan to bear. The promise that he would never turn his back on her; was precisely the vow he failed to keep when he intentionally and decisively turned away from her time and again. He held her firm and raised her head until he was able to gaze into her eyes, "Molly." He was inexplicably powerless to find the words to tell her how remorseful and repentant he was. He stood stagnant while the fierce drops of rain gushed unapologetically down his face. He wanted to tell her a million times over how sorry he was, but he was convinced that nothing he could say, would ever recover Molly's crushed heart. She anxiously lingered, hoping that he would say something, but when she realized he had nothing to say, she turned away from him.

Ryan was grudgingly caught up in mammoth divergence with himself as he unhurriedly drove back to his apartment, virtually without purpose or resolution. His mind ordered him to choose between the two significant women in his life, while his heart instructed him to surrender to Molly. For the first time since Molly had returned home, he was ready to declare that he still loved her, and that he was determined to battle for her, and for what they once had. The words that she carelessly attacked him with earlier, were playing out over and over in his mind, at the same time, he decisively knew that the performance was finally over, and that the curtain had ultimately come down. They could no longer persist in this tireless and exhaustive manner. It was up to Ryan to mend the broken fences with both Molly and Flo.

When he strolled into his apartment, he noticed that Flo had taken down her luggage while neatly folding the scattered clothing on their bed. "Hey, are you okay?" She walked over to Ryan when she found him standing despondently in the doorway. Ryan sobbed despairingly into Flo's arms while admitting to feeling defeated and overwhelmed. "She didn't?" "No, she didn't." Flo turned back to their bed and commenced with the sorting and packing her clothes. "Flo." He had a burning desire to explain himself to her. Flo gazed at him with warmth in her eyes and smiled sadly at him. "Ryan, you don't love me, not like that, and that's fine. Honestly, I am fine with that. You are a great man, and you deserve to be really happy. And I think, I think that's what Molly wanted to do, you know? Make you happy. I believe she thought that the baby might come between us. She loves you, Ryan. Don't you understand that it was her love for you that drove her to do it in the first place? And, you adore her, something about the way you look at her, if I had that ..." "Flo."

Ryan was desperate to let Flo know that he never planned for their lives to turn out as it did. "No Ryan, you are bringing a child into this world. You've got one more last chance, and you have a desperate need for this baby. And, do you know why? You can't stand to be away from her, and again, that's okay, because it is the one way to keep her in your life. And Ryan, I love you enough to give you that one last chance."

Flo zipped up her suitcases before she hugged him firmly. She sympathetically whispered goodbye to him, and sorrowfully closed the apartment door behind her. Ryan felt immeasurable guilt towards Flo, but it was Molly he could no longer deny.

Molly had shut herself out from the outside world and spent the afternoon sleeping after she had returned from the medical center, desperate to process all that had transpired between her and Ryan. When she awoke earlier in the evening, just as the sun was setting, she felt unpredictably invigorated and unexpectedly optimistic at the prospect of becoming a mother for the very first time.

Shortly after eight the evening, Molly turned on the radio, hopeful that the annual Christmas carol marathon was still in full swing. Even though Christmas had come to an end, she had a fraught desire to cling to a speculative belief that there would be a miracle out there somewhere, unwearyingly, and tolerantly in anticipation of her. For the first time since Molly could remember, it no longer felt to her as though her heart was in tatters or battered, as it had been only just recently. Molly cheerfully sang along while reminiscing over all she had loved and cherished. She sorrowfully recalled those she had lost along the way. She pensively and dreamily placed her hand on her belly, and inadvertently whispered a silent prayer for her baby. She prayed that she would be mercifully absolved from what she had done years before, while she thanked God for intervening when she was about to make the same reprehensible mistake once again. Ryan would never discard or banish her, even though she would have to learn to live with his resentment. At the same time, she would have to teach herself to accept that Flo would remain steadfast behind Ryan.

Above the tunes chiming from her radio, Molly heard a soft, but audible knock on her front door. She timidly turned down the volume, and diffidently made her way to the front door. She was staggered and stunned to unexpectedly find Ryan standing there, and it baffled her vastly when Flo failed to identify herself. "Can I come in?" Ryan was carrying a brightly wrapped gift under his arm. "Where's Flo?" Molly glanced around once again. "She's gone, she's left …" Ryan handed her the gift. "Left? Like in gone?" Molly was instantly perplexed. "Yeah, we, it wasn't going to work anyway." "Why not? Is it because of the baby?"

Molly

"It's not the baby, Molly, it's you." He was anxious to enforce the understanding that it was in no way at all about the baby that had capriciously come into their lives. "Flo knew all along that, that I didn't love her the way she wanted me to. I guess she thought that the longer we were together, that I might love her the way I once loved you. Do you know what she said to me tonight?" Ryan let out a poignant snigger. "She said that I still loved you, and that I was using the baby as an excuse to be closer to you. She also said that I never look at her the way I look at you." Molly perfunctorily sat down beside him, and urgently sought to find corroboration in his eyes. "Why would she say that?" "I guess it's because, I do still love you, Molly." Ryan took her trembling hands into his. "Ryan?" Molly's heart had instantly skipped a beat. Not once had she considered a reality in which Ryan would ever profess his love to her again. "Molly, all this time I thought I was mad at you, instead, I am so livid with myself for letting you go, and letting you go through the baby on your own." "Ryan, it's nobody's fault. I've spoken to my dad ..." Molly was about to reassure him that it was not any one person's burden to carry. "Yeah, me too." Ryan nodded as if in a daze. "You spoke to my father?" "Yeah, I had to get it off my chest, and I guess he did it because he loved you, you're his little girl. I know he's sorry, Molly, but I just can't seem to understand why he had so little faith in me. He thought that he was being a good father, you know?" Ryan paused to take in a deep breath, "I know this is a gamble, and I know that perhaps I'm asking too much of you, but please can you forgive me?" "Ryan." Molly clasped his face in her hands, "Ryan." "Yeah, I know, too much has happened. I know I can't change what's happened and what has been said, but I'd like a chance to try. We were meant to be together. You must know that Mols?" He bowed his head desolately. "I know that you'll come back to me, Molly, and I can wait for you. I can wait a million years for you if that is what it takes." He lifted himself from the sofa before he gently kissed her on her brow. "And, even if it takes a million years, we will have the baby." Ryan strolled out her front door just as swiftly as he had walked in, and while Molly stood watching him, she was fraught to absorb all he had said to her only moments before.

She turned back to the living room and was wholeheartedly aware of a gigantic smile that had snuck up on her face. She felt as though a weight had lifted from her heart, and she was tempted to shout out after him that she loved him too. But she had to proceed with caution. Time had placed an enormous amount of distance between them. They had moved from love to hate and back to love in such a short time, that Molly remained indisputably cautious of her relationship with Ryan. She adored and cherished him, and she was convinced that they could work their faults out, even if it took forever. She slowly

Molly

unwrapped the gift he had left behind for her and was delighted to find that it was an album he had put together of while they were growing up. He had left many blank pages, and Molly instinctively understood that he was trying to tell her that all would be alright again, and that they would soon fill up the empty pages with brand new memories.

Alice VL

A THOUSAND SMILES

As was typical for the weeks following Christmas, Ryan pitched up at Molly's place at the break of dawn as he did on so many mornings before. He made a valiant effort to check in on her in daily, first thing as the sun was about to rise, and once again as the sun was about to set. She routinely invited him inside and poured each a mug of coffee before they jointly made their way out to the terrace. After they had sat in stillness that specific morning, Ryan turned to face her with a downcast look in his eyes. "Molly, I worry about you here, on your own, and it's tricky for me to be constantly close to you with you living here, and me over there. I know that things have been jagged...and I know, I know we haven't really been getting along lately, but come and live with me, just for a while, just till after the baby is born?" Molly stared at Ryan in disbelief while attempting to fathom what he was asking of her, but suspicious of the fact that it might not be the best situation for them. "I don't know, Ryan?" "Molly, I'll give you your space. I have enough room, if that's what you're worried about? You'll have your own bedroom." He was restlessly challenged, while fervently determined to persuade her that it would be the perfect answer for her and for the baby. "I'm always going to worry about you, and I just want to know that you and the baby are okay, please? Just until after the baby comes. Anything can go wrong, and you'll be here on your own. Let me be there this time, give me the chance I never had the last time?" Molly unwittingly gazed at him. His gentle demeanor reminded her of the boy she fell in love with almost a lifetime ago. It swept her back to all the promises they had once made to one another, and it provided her with optimism that some of their dreams could perhaps still come true. "Alright, Ryan, but just for a while." Ryan let out a sigh of reprieve while abundantly aware that it would present him with one last opening to reacquaint and reconnect with her again. It was an opportunity to discover and revise all about her, all over again as though it would be for the very first time. They were both unrecognizably distorted to one another, but he was certain that she still loved him, while he in turn, was frantic at the prospect of proving his untainted and haunting love for her one more time.

He helped Molly pack her personal belongings, and promptly closed up and locked down the townhouse on her behalf. He swore to her that he would drop in daily to ensure that her plants were watered, and that the housekeeper was let in as per her schedule. Wandering through her townhouse one last time, he decided straight away that Molly was deserving of so much more. When they reached his apartment only a few minutes later, Ryan was in high spirits and animated to lead the way for Molly. After placing her bags in the spare bedroom, Ryan was instantly at ease and relieved that she had agreed to come and live with him.

He prized having Molly close by, satisfied that he could watch her closer. It was all he had ever hunted after, and it was all he could ever think of from the moment he recognized that he couldn't subsist without her. Molly stood gazing out over the ocean while Ryan hid in the background, powerless to stop staring at her, or rebuff her beauty. He appreciated the vision of her growing belly and was astounded by his emotions when he watched her standing there. He closed his eyes and was once more enormously indebted for the opportunity to be visible for her, and their baby. He felt tremendous guilt over choosing Flo, and for forcing Molly to endure the distress of witnessing his correlation with another woman. He was enormously remorseful for putting her through the anguish and torment, but he made a secret oath to spend the rest of his life convincing her that there would never again be another woman who could lay a claim to his heart.

Ryan was jolted back to reality when he heard Molly's virtually muffled murmur, "Goodnight, Ryan." "Goodnight,

Molly, if you need anything, just shout." After indulging in a temperate bath, Molly turned off the lights, and climbed into her bed. She lay gawping at the ceiling, while sensitive to the fact that Ryan was just one door away from her, a recognition and realization that once again enforced feelings of safety. When Ryan turned in for the night, he quietly checked in on Molly who had fallen asleep earlier. He delicately moved closer to her, and he wondered if it was possible to worship her more than he did at that very instant. Watching her sleep so serenely, made it almost intolerable for Ryan to reflect on all she had suffered in such a short time. Molly was delicate and fragile, and he could barely shake a nudging feeling that he had almost broken her into a million pieces. Ryan wanted more than anything to slide in beside her and hold her firmly in his arms all night long. He was frenetic to promise her that he would take care of her just as he had sworn to her when they were just children, but at the same time, he was agonizingly aware of the fact that Molly had listened to that exact same conversation once before.

When he crawled into his own bed, Ryan lay thinking about her again, unable to get her out of his mind or fall asleep. The vision of her sleeping haunted him, and he could hardly settle on how he could have been as foolish as to let her go, again and again. He thought back to all the occasions where he was responsible for her tears, while unenthusiastically accepting that the hurt in her eyes would disturb him for a while to come. It occurred to him that it had been ages since he had seen her smile, and he unsuccessfully tried to remember a time when he could recall her being nothing but happy.

He awoke to sudden movement in the bedroom next door before he hurriedly glanced over at the alarm clock on his pedestal. When Ryan realized that it was only moments after three the morning, he was convinced that something was worryingly and unquestionably wide of the mark with Molly. Before he could get out of his bed to check up on her, he noticed her unexpectedly standing in the doorway of his bedroom. "Molly?" She cautiously moved closer to him. He at once noticed her tears that had begun to roll down her cheeks. "What's wrong?" He instantly leaped from his bed. "Ryan, I didn't want to wake you. I just, please will you just hold me?" He confidently placed his arms around her and held her protectively against him. "What's the matter?" He retreated for just an instant. "Nothing." She held him firmer against him. "Is it the baby?" "No, I'm just scared, Ryan." "Why? What are you scared of?" "I don't know. I just am." Molly was at once utterly baffled by her own emotions. "Oh, Molly, you're going to be fine. Come, lay here next to me." He exposed the other side of the bed for her, before Molly crawled in slowly, and turned her back on him. He slid in next to her and held her steadfastly in his arms. Molly was sheltered once again. She was confident that she only needed to feel his arms around her. He lay close to her, trying to take in all about her as he remembered the little things that had elapsed along the way. He adored her scent, and when he detected that she had fallen asleep, he laid closer to her. "I love you, Molly, forever and always."

Ryan awoke to the exasperating and deafening bleeping of the alarm clock the following morning. He peered over to Molly but was horrified to find that she was no longer in his bed. He swiftly ran down the passage, and felt acute panic seize his heart. When he reached the living room, he noticed her seated out on the terrace, a blanket snugly covering her. "Molly?" "These sunrises ..." "You scared me, when I woke up, and you weren't there." She gazed up at him and smiled lovingly. "So, Molly, I've got some business in town later, will you be okay on your own for a while?" "I'll be fine Ryan, really." He kissed her on the cheek and disappeared back into his bedroom.

Ryan rushed through the shower, zealously aware of the exhilaration building up inside of him at the prospect of what he had planned that day. It was colossal, and it was an enormous surprise for Molly. It would finally convince her of how much he cherished her, and how euphoric he was that she had returned to him, starting a family with him. When he was dressed and ready to leave, he kissed Molly swiftly, and promised her that he would make a concerted effort to return before sundown.

Molly gazed at him as he walked out the door, and for the first time in her entire life, her heart was no longer threatened or fearful of whether or not he would return to her. She knew into her core, that Ryan Neves would always come back for Molly Starkey.

Alice VL

Molly

Ryan spent the majority of the morning visiting houses with two separate real estate agents. He was intent on finding the perfect home for Molly and their baby, a brand-new house to start a brand-new life in. He greatly hunted Molly to continue writing her novels, so that she could remain close to him and their child. He was searching for a place that she could call home, and feel protected and secured in, at all times. Ryan viewed countless houses during his search but failed to find the single house that felt like home to him. On his way to the next viewing, he passed a house that instantaneously and without expectation, took his breath away. The house was not for sale, but he had a sudden and impulsive urge to learn more about the dwelling.

Ryan apprehensively walked up the path to the front door while probing himself as to how he would successfully implore the owners and convince them to sell him their home. When he frivolously knocked on the front door, Ryan had no indication as to how to initiate the conversation and attempt to explain to them how crucial it was to give his family the home of their dreams. It was a beautiful house, and by the plate that was cemented onto the wall at the front door, Ryan was astounded to discover that the building dated back to the eighteenth century. Ryan was effusively sensitive to how profoundly Molly acclaimed all ancient and old. He instinctively knew precisely how great her passion would be for this house. "Yes?" An old man greeted him almost right away. "Hello, my name is Ryan Neves …" Ryan hurriedly and tensely introduced himself, while extending an open hand out to the old man. "Wilbur Rice." He gallantly shook Ryan's hand. "Mr. Rice, I don't know how to ask you this, and you're probably going to think I'm a mad man, maybe I should just first start by saying that you have a beautiful home." "Thank you, son?" "Mr. Rice, I have this, this most amazing woman in my life, and I really messed things up with her along the way. Anyway, what I'm trying to say is, we're going to have a baby, and I really want to get her a fresh start, a home for new beginnings. I've looked at so many houses, but it was yours that just took my breath away. If you knew what she has been through, maybe you would consider, maybe you would just think about selling me your house?" Mr. Rice smiled, before he made way for Ryan to enter. "Well then, you'd better come on inside." He cheerfully invited Ryan into his home.

Ryan followed the old man indoors, and swiftly glanced around him. Without an ounce of hesitation in Ryan's mind, he was convinced that Wilbur Rice's home had to become their home. He showed Ryan to an empty seat in the kitchen, before he took a seat directly across from him. "Funny thing, I was going to put this house on the market years ago, but I could never bring myself to actually do it." He bowed his head, and lightly shook it. "My wife died a while back, and this place has become too large for me. But, letting it go is just so hard. All our children were born here, but none of them want this old place." He offered Ryan a little bit of narration on the house he had brought his bride home to, and watched his children born into. "I knew that I would know when the time is right, and it seems to me that the time has come." Ryan smirked with relief and after agreeing on a suitable selling price and the availability of the house, Ryan left just as swiftly as he had walked in, positive that he had done the right thing. His heart promised him that they could finally begin again.

During his drive back home to Molly, Ryan was ardently aware of the exhilaration that had begun to engulf him. He thought about Molly and their baby and was thrilled with the idea of surprising her with an outfitted nursery for their child. Ryan reminded himself to discuss the baby's gender with Molly, but he questioned whether it was truly crucial to know. As he was about to turn into the apartment composite, he was brought back to reality by the sudden ringing of his phone. From the caller identity, he realized at once that it was Louis on the other end, "Hey buddy!" "Hey Ryan, what's up?" "Just on my way home." "All right so, Ida wants to know if you guys want to come over for dinner tonight?" "Yeah, that'd be great. Let me speak to Molly and I'll call you back." Louis frowned, sure that he had meant Flo instead of Molly. "You mean Flo?" Ryan burst out laughing, "No, I mean Molly." He brusquely ended the call when he reached the apartment before rushing through the front door. As was usual, Molly was blissfully trapped in a total diverse world while behind her notebook, oblivious to the world around her. "Hey." "Hi." Molly was instantly elated to see him. "What are you doing?" Ryan peered over her shoulders. "I'm trying to figure this internet and email thingy out." "Ida has invited us over for supper, do you want to go?" "Sure, that would be great, I miss her." Ryan speedily called Louis and confirmed their dinner plans. Ryan walked over to the fridge and brought two glasses of lemonade back with him. "Listen, Molly, can we talk?" Ryan handed her a glass. "Sure." She shut her notebook at once. "We've never discussed this before, and I'm not sure how you'd feel about it, but wouldn't you like to know if the baby was a boy or a girl?" "I've never thought about it. I suppose it would be nice to know? Why do you ask?" "Oh, no reason really, I was just wondering?" "Well, I've got to be at the doctors on Thursday. We can always ask him then?" Ryan gazed back at her and beamed at the very notion while nodding in approval. "So, what did you do today?" "Oh, not much. My publisher wants me to send chapters by email, and it's all too technologically challenging for me. What happened to good old-fashioned pen and paper?" Ryan chortled out loud at her obvious disgust with the new and was once again reminded of how much she cherished the old.

The sun had barely begun to set when they arrived at

Alice VL

Louis and Ida's home. Molly was expectedly upset to learn that Piper had gone to bed earlier than usual. "Oh, she's a little off, a rotten tonsil infection." "Poor thing." Louis and Ryan made their way to the dining room while Molly followed Ida into the kitchen. "So, Molly, Louis says you're living with Ryan?" "Yeah, but not *with* him, only at his place and besides, it's only temporary, just until the baby comes." Ida glared at Molly in reprehension and utter disbelief, "Oh come on Ida, nothing's going on." "Yeah, right!" Ida smiled covertly. "I haven't seen you this happy in a long time. Your eyes are sparkling again, and I know that it has everything to do with Ryan!" "I must admit, it's nice having him around me again." Molly gushed bashfully, "but, we have our own bedrooms, in case you were wondering." Ida shook her head rigorously and grinned from ear to ear, suspicious of their so-called partition. She had always known that Ryan and Molly could never keep their hands off one another, and she knew that it was just a matter of time before Molly's world collides with Ryan's again.

Louis and Ryan were setting the dinner table at the same time as pouring generous amounts of wine to enjoy with their supper. "Listen buddy, no wine for Molly please." "Oh, right." Louis hurriedly replaced her goblet of wine with a glass of Lemonade, "So, how are things with Molly there?" "Oh man, its great!" Louis was unambiguously aware of the enthusiasm in his friend's voice. "There were so many things about her that I had forgotten, and it's, it's so amazing to see these little things again, you know? Like I'm seeing it again for the very first time." "I take it you guys are working things out?" "No, not like that." "Oh, come on, Ryan!" "No, honestly, and it's not that I don't want to." "What makes you think you'll be able to, you know? I mean, you guys did it since the age of what, fifteen or something?" "You know, buddy? It's just not that important to me anymore." "Don't worry about it, pal, we'll see how long it lasts." Louis broke out into spontaneous laughter, while patting Ryan on his back. "What are you two laughing about?" Ida brought in the food with Molly on her heels. "Oh, nothing, just stuff." Ryan became embarrassed almost at once. Molly smiled at him when she realized how mortified he had become all of a sudden. She was certain that they were quite possibly on the same topic as she and Ida were on. Molly took her place next to Ryan, and promptly found his hand under the table before she affectionately squeezed it. Ryan gazed at Molly while thinking about what Louis had said earlier, and unintentionally, evoked their one night together not too long ago. Louis and Ida glanced at one another and smiled enthusiastically when they noticed the silent exchange between their friends. "So." Ryan was at once anxious to break the silence, "We're going to find out whether the baby is a boy or a girl." "Really?" Ida was caught off-guard, "Wouldn't you rather want to be surprised?" "I think I've had enough surprises in my life, thanks Ida." Molly responded in haste. Ryan became quiet when he thought of all the shockers that had crept up on Molly, surprises that he was sure, she would rather forget.

They had only moments before concluded their dinner when Molly felt queasy and promptly excused herself. She told Ryan that she was keen to step outside for a bout of fresh air, and that she was sensitive to the unanticipated claustrophobia she was suddenly prone to. Ryan smiled warmly, aware of the persistent nausea that struck relentlessly, and was anxious for her to recover sooner rather than later. While assisting Ida and Louis clear the dinner table, he held up his index finger against his lips in an attempt to indicate ambiguity to his friends. When he was sure that Molly could not at all hear them, he promptly turned back to his friends. "Listen, while we're alone, I did the most amazing thing today." Ryan became animated straight away, "I bought a new house! Well, an old, new house!" "Oh, wow!" Ida was stunned at the revelation. "Yeah, but I need your help, Ida. I want to make sure everything is perfect before I take her there. She doesn't know anything. I want to surprise her." He rambled on in one breath while peering over his shoulders often, nervous that Molly might walk in on their conversation. "Ida, I need your help with the baby's room." "So, that's why you want to know!" Before she could respond, Molly leisurely strolled in, and was at once certain that she detected guilt and culpability in each of their eyes. Awkwardly, they stood gaping at her in silence. "What?" "Nothing, we're just washing up." Ida responded with haste before she carried on loading the dirty dishes into the washer, desperately trying to avoid eye contact with her.

Alice VL

Molly

When they arrived back home, Molly at once indulged in a warm bath, and lay simmering for what seemed like hours. She noticed that her belly was growing larger, and it reconfirmed the authenticity of the new life she was carrying inside of her. She instinctively questioned whether Ryan thought her to be beautiful, and sullenly compared herself to an elephant. She thought back to dinner with Louis and Ida, and immensely appreciated the fact that it was their first dinner together, without her and Ryan at war with one another. She recalled Ryan's expression when he gazed at her during dinner, and she once again realized how insufferably intricate it was for her to maintain adequate aloofness from him. It was tremendously frustrating for her to be as close to him, unable to take his hand or embrace him freely. Once more, she longed for the days where she could cuddle him any time she wanted to.

When she had slipped on her nightgown, she made her way to the kitchen where she ran into Ryan who had just come in from the terrace, "Ryan?" "Hey, I was just admiring the sky tonight." He gently took Molly by the hand, "Come, let's go to bed." Molly again crawled in next to him, but this time, she didn't turn away from him. They lay staring at one another in silence, each wondering where they were headed for, and how it would all work out for them. "Did you ever think things would turn out like this?" Ryan turned onto his back and faced the ceiling, "No, I thought things would've been much easier for us." He whispered dolefully. "Yeah, me too. Ryan. Will you, will you make love to me?" Ryan turned back to face her and smiled amorously. "Molly, I know being pregnant isn't easy, but I also know that you're feeling a little vulnerable at the moment, and right now, I don't want to make things harder for you, or do something you might regret tomorrow." He was aching for her, and each time he caught a glimpse of her, he had to remind himself that he considered it direly necessary to allow her the legroom he was certain she needed. Molly felt tears well up inside of her, once again aware of how agonizing Ryan's denunciation was. "Molly don't cry. I want to, you have no idea how much I want to. I just, I just don't want to screw up again. I love you, I do." He held her steadily against him. "I love you, Molly."

Molly

Alice VL

HOME

Ryan had been spending his afternoons and evenings clandestinely organizing and preparing the new house for Molly. They discovered that the baby they were having was expected to be a healthy little girl. Ryan at once roped Ida in to assist with organizing the whole lot before their little girl showed up. It was intricate to keep their comings and goings hidden from Molly, out of fear that she may become suspicious of them. There were instances when Ryan ran out of excuses to come up with each time, he left the apartment. He lied to her consistently. Molly knew him well enough to know that he was being dishonest to her about his whereabouts. When she tallied up how regularly he was out at night and how often he had lied to her about his comings and goings, she recognized the inhospitable and unsolicited feelings of diffidence and uncertainty that had begun to pester her yet again. She was positive that Ryan found her repulsive and sordid, swayed that he was secretly cavorting another woman. She was effusively aware of the certainty that their living arrangement was temporary, and it worried her terrifically when her mind convinced her she was about to lose

Molly

Ryan again. At night, Ryan purely cuddled her until they both had fallen asleep, and by the way he held her at night, Molly's heart reassured her of his love for her, but her mind refused to corroborate and play along. Molly was positive that he was keeping secrets from her, and she was extremely mindful to the appearance of his mind drifting off more often than before. She felt as though they were living past one another, and it terrified her to admit that they may in no way at all, be who they once were.

Ryan arrived home just before midnight one harrowing night to find Molly distressingly convinced that he was caught up in his lover's arms. He was certain she would be asleep but was staggered to find her unexpectedly sitting out on the terrace. "Molly, what's the matter?" He removed his jacket and placed it around her shoulders. "It's cold out here." When Molly turned to face him, he at once became anxious when he found her sobbing. "Why am I here, Ryan?" "Hey, where's this coming from?" "No Ryan, why am I really here?" "Molly, you know why?" "I'm only pregnant, Ryan, not stupid!" "Molly, calm down." He tried to take her hands into his. When she abruptly retreated from him, Ryan was bemused once again. "I know that I'm fat, and ugly, and I am fully aware of what I look like, but you're never here. I never see you anymore. You leave me alone nearly all day, and you come back so late at night. I thought that the whole point of me living here was so that, so that I wouldn't be alone. I rather, I rather want to go back to my place." Molly became panicky and began choking on her words. "Molly?" Ryan moved cautiously closer to her. "No, leave me alone! I know there's someone else." "Wait, you don't think, do you think?" He suddenly exploded into a fit of laughter. "What's so funny?" "Molly," He leaned forward, and took her in his arms. "There's no-one else, Molly, only you." "I don't believe you. Where do you go each day?" "I'll tell you what, put something warm on, and I'll go show you."

Molly was at once unsettled when they reached an unfamiliar house, and wasn't at all sure where they were, yet baffled as to why Ryan had brought her there. "Where are we, Ryan?" "Shhh, we don't want to wake anybody." He opened up the car door for her to climb out. "I don't understand?" He took her by her hand and led her up the path towards the enormous front doors. "Ryan, who lives here?" Ryan disregarded her questions and took out a set of keys from his pocket. When he unlocked the front door, Ryan gently pushed it open, and made way for her to enter. She nervously glanced around in silence, afraid of waking the owners she was convinced, were sound asleep. "Ryan, we can't just walk in?" She whispered almost inaudibly when Ryan joined her in the entrance hall. "Molly, it's only you, it's always only been you." He devotedly swept her into his arms. "This is where I've been coming everyday Molly, and so has Ida and Louis." By the expression on her face, Ryan was convinced that Molly was utterly confused and completely disoriented. "I wanted to surprise you, and with the baby coming, I just thought that we needed a bigger place." Molly abruptly stepped back from him, and hurriedly glanced around her. "This is, for us?" "No Molly, this is for *you,* and if you'll have me?"

They ambled from room to room without uttering a sound. While glancing around her, Molly was brilliantly aware of how rigidly Ryan had worked on their new home. He gently took her hand and led her upstairs into the nursery. Molly was bowled over when he invited her inside. She appreciated once more how great an effort Ryan had placed into bringing her home, and it reduced her to unexpected and unforeseen tears. She turned to him when she began to weep, recalling how she fallaciously accused him of rendezvousing with another woman, when in fact, what he was essentially doing, was creating a home for them. "I can't believe you did all this. I feel so stupid now, Ryan, I am so sorry." Ryan smiled graciously when he noticed the look of approval on her face. His heart and his mind came together to confirm that it was worth each long night, and every early morning. There was no indication, nothing to prepare him for the expression in Molly's eyes. It took his breath away to witness her as contented as she was at that very moment. Ryan was convinced that he would never forget the way she looked that night. Without saying another word, he took her by her hand, and led her into their brand-new bedroom. Molly gasped for air when she peered inside and stood in bewilderment once again while glancing around her. There was nothing that came to mind that could articulate how truly beautiful it all was, and how exceedingly indebted Molly felt to Ryan at that very minute. The look on her face told him a thousand stories that night, but the confirmation that he so direly needed that he for once, had done right by Molly, was all he ever sought after. He took her hand once again, and led her to their new, oversized bed where he laid her down tenderly. While wiping the tears of joy from her eyes, he gradually undressed her, before he started to kiss her avidly. Molly had patiently waited for this night for longer than she could remember, and she shut her eyes firmly while Ryan gently made love to her.

RYAN'S GIRL

Without warning, Piper's birthday had rolled around once again, and the reality of Piper growing up horrified Molly, reducing her tears more often than not. Piper adored Molly's growing belly, and never tired of touching it while endlessly thrilled to feel the baby move around. After they had moved into their new home, Ryan and Molly spent a great deal more time together. They took pleasure in quiet nights in their new home, the home that Molly cherished wholeheartedly. They would lay into the early hours of the morning reminiscing about their lives together as children, and the twist their lives had taken when they were older. Even though they had gradually found their way into one another's hearts again, Ryan could hardly shake the feeling that Molly continued to linger with reservations about his love for her. He was desperate for Molly to become his wife, and although he was often tempted to remind her that she once swore to marry him, out of trepidation of blemishing, he dawdled.

"Where's my big girl?" Piper breathlessly ran up to Molly, "Aunty Molly can't pick you up, sweetie, remember the baby in her tummy?" Ida reminded her daughter who had flung her arms around Molly. "I'm sorry, Princess, but soon, okay?" After handing Piper her birthday gift, they all made their way indoors. "I feel like an elephant." Ida was instantly aware of how enormously uncomfortable Molly had become. "Is Ryan here yet?" Molly grimaced. "No, I thought you guys were coming together. He said that he was going to pick you up?" "Shit Ida, I forgot!" Molly reached for her mobile phone straight away. As she was about to make the call to Ryan, her phone rang, "Ryan?" "Molly? Where are you?" "Sorry Ryan, I forgot that you were going to pick me up. I'm at Ida's already." "I told you I didn't want you driving, Molly. I'll be there in a minute." He abruptly ended the call. "Gees Ida, I'm only pregnant, not sick!" "He worries about you Molly, because he loves you." "So, listen, Molly, are you and Ryan, you know?" "No, not really, not like that. We're taking it slow. I just don't think that Ryan is ready to put the past behind him just yet?" She became gloomy almost at once. "I mean...he says that things will get better, but I can't help but feel that he hasn't completely forgiven me, you know?" She let out a faint sigh, "I thought that maybe when we moved into the house, that things might change and that he might want to get married, but the subject just never came up?" Molly became silent when Louis joined them.

"You know, Molly, Ryan couldn't forget you," She gazed

Alice VL

at Louis with sorrow in her eyes when he interrupted her. "Molly, do you know why Ryan came back?" He took her hands into his, and gently stroked them. "He came back for you. I don't care how profusely he denies it, in all the years that I have known Ryan, he has never looked at anybody in the same way he looks at you. Ryan was a muddle when you called to, well, to tell him that it was over, and he tried his utmost to find you. He wanted to look you in the eye when you told him that it was over. We all knew that he had your future all planned out, and he couldn't wait for the day that you came back to him. When you didn't come back, Ryan couldn't go on Molly, and he was so sure that he had lost you forever." Molly grew sadder when Louis carried on explaining. "When he found out about, about the abortion, it nearly killed him. He just couldn't understand why you had done it, and even though we tried to tell him, tried to explain, he wouldn't listen. When Flo came along, Ida and I knew that he was trying to hurt you, but at the same time, we also knew that he wanted you back. We've always known that you guys are no good without the other."

Molly swabbed at a lost tear that had rolled down her cheek. "Hey, where's the birthday girl?" They were instantly alert to Ryan call out when he arrived, "I'm here!" Piper ran up to him before she flung herself into his arms. Molly glanced over at Ryan and was positive that they were plunged back together for a reason. She was confident that there was nothing that could stand in their way of happiness and bliss any longer. Ryan turned to Molly, and gently kissed her on the cheek. He was the only man she had ever been with, and there was no-one else that she would rather share her body, mind, and soul with. She realized once again that she loved him more than anything else in the world, but at times, she was terrified of what might lay ahead for them.

"Shall we go out to the pool?" Louis took Ryan by his arm and turned to the direction of the pool. "Yeah, sure." Ryan restlessly turned back to Molly. "Are you feeling okay? You look a little pale?" "I'm fine, just scorching and uncomfortable, that's all." She turned to Ida. "Let's go sit outside with them." "Molly, are you sure you are really alright? Ryan is right, you do look a little pale." Ida scowled uneasily. "Yes, what's with you guys?" Just as they reached the pool, Molly paused for a moment, "Oh darn, I forgot my water. I'm just going to pour myself a glass, I'll be just a moment." Molly turned to go back into the house. When she began climbing the small number of stairs into the house, she unexpectedly felt as though her belly was being grasped and squeezed with two hands. She was unfamiliar with the sensation, and instinctively knew that something was wide of the mark. When the twinge receded, she hurriedly poured herself a glass of water. She was barely able to lift the glass to her mouth, when she gasped for breath, terrifyingly aware of the pain that had ruthlessly returned. Louis and Ryan were standing around the barbeque when they heard glass shatter from inside the house. Ryan scrammed to reach her, with Louis and Ida not far behind him. Molly was almost on her knees when they reached her, "Molly?" Ryan moved hesitantly towards her. "Ryan, something's wrong?" "Oh shit, her water broke!" Ida ran down the passage, and immediately returned with a towel. Molly turned back to Ryan, "Ryan?" He took her by her arm, and for a moment, he had struck a total and complete blank. Ida shoved the towel into Molly's hands, and yelled out to Ryan, "Take her to the hospital!" "It's going to be okay, Molly, just hang in there." Ryan shoved her into the car, and speedily pulled out of the driveway. They had hardly climbed onto the route to the hospital when Molly was again aware of the excruciating pain build up inside of her, this time, it had mercilessly spread into her back.

"Ryan, help me please!" She cried out to him in agony. "We're almost there, Molly, please just hold on." He made an extraordinary and valiant effort to remain composed and unruffled as they turned into the hospital. Molly was thankful that the pain didn't last, but each time it revisited her, it felt to her as though it was a hundred times worse than only moments before.

Alice VL

Molly

They had only moments earlier entered the maternity ward when Molly faced Ryan and noticed panic and uncertainty in his eyes. "Are you okay, Molly? Please tell me you're alright?" Molly had only just managed a weak smile through the contractions, "Please help me!" She was promptly supported by a horde of nurses and helped onto an empty bed. An on-call doctor approached her with urgency, and speedily examined her, "It's not long now, you're nearly there, just one hard push." Ryan held onto Molly while she horrendously moaned with her last push, and in a matter of seconds, they could hear their baby cry. Without indignity, Ryan allowed his tears to flow liberally and unreservedly from his cheeks, while holding Molly affectionately in his arms.

"My baby." Molly contemplated as she gaped at her little girl, calmly lying in the arms of a nurse. "She's so beautiful, Molly." Ryan took his daughter and gently placed her in Molly's arms. She was in awe of her little baby girl as she stared desolately at her. She gazed up at Ryan and noticed the instant love for his daughter reflect in his eyes, "I'm so sorry, Ryan, for what I did." "It's over Molly, let's put that behind us. We have a brand-new baby girl to take care of and love, and I wouldn't trade her for any other baby." Ryan patiently waited for the doctor and nurses to leave before he turned back to Molly, "Molly, I love you, and …" He began to stumble slightly before he pulled a ring from his pocket, the same ring he had given her so many years ago. "I know I can't make right what happened between us, and I know, I know I can't take back the things I said to you, but I want to spend the rest of my life with you, and I want to be able to raise our daughter as a family." He paused nervously, "Don't you know by now that nothing else matters to me? I love you, Molly, I love you. Will you please marry me?" For the second time in Molly's life, Ryan placed the same ring on her finger. Molly smiled sorrowfully, and gently touched his face, "Yes, Ryan, I thought you'd never ask. You know, she needs a name?" Molly gently stroked her daughter's cheek. "Yeah, how about Molly?" "Oh no!" She burst out laughing. "No way!" "How about Riley?" "Riley?" "For Ryan and Molly?" "Perfect." Molly unexpectedly burst out crying. "She was born on Piper's birthday, isn't that such a beautiful blessing?" Ryan smiled sadly and kissed her on her forehead.

He kissed them both and turned to leave, leaving Molly mystified in the midst of his abrupt departure. While he walked out, she turned her attention back to baby Riley, "My princess …" Ryan instantly met Louis and Ida outside the ward, "It's a girl!" He smirked while Louis and Ida had tears of joy streaming from their eyes. "On Piper's birthday! Oh Ryan, that's wonderful. Are they okay?" Ida embraced him, and hurriedly dried the tears on her cheeks. "They're fine. She is beautiful and bouncy and happy and healthy!" Ryan could not at all contain his exhilaration. "So, Ida, did you do what I asked you this morning when I called?" "Oh yes! Yes, they're on their way. As a matter of fact, they should be here …" Ida became silent when she noticed the Starkey family walk in. "Mr. Starkey, Mrs. Starkey, Tyron and Megan! Thank you so much for coming, Molly has no idea, I didn't tell her." Ryan nervously welcomed Molly's family. "Son, can you ever forgive me? I should've known better." James resolutely embraced Ryan. "I have Molly back, and that's all that matters, it's all that will ever matter." He firmly shook James' hand. "Anyway, it's a girl, healthy and beautiful!" Ryan announced while embracing Molly's mother. "Congratulations son! Can we see her?" James was instantly anxious to see his daughter and in a hurry to meet his grand-daughter for the very first time. "Yeah, through there." Molly was brooding incessantly over her baby girl, when from the corner of her eyes, she thought she noticed Ryan walking back in, "Ryan, come look here," She whispered before she turned to face him.

Her heart began to shudder and race all at the same time, and she was once again reduced to tears. Molly realized that there was nothing any one person could accomplish at that very moment to ensure her day's utmost and undeniable perfection. "Mommy, daddy!" She held out her arms to them as her tears rolled unreservedly from her eyes. "Hello, my girl!" James Starkey held onto his daughter, overcome with joy and sadness, all at the same time. "Hello, baby." Sue instantly turned her attention to their brand-new granddaughter. "Oh, she's so beautiful, Molly." Sue took her into her arms for the very first time. "How did you know?" Molly gazed questioningly at her father. "Ryan called yesterday and asked us to come. He told us about the baby, and I knew, we just had to be here. Ida made all the arrangements for us to get here. This is our first grandchild. She's beautiful, my girl." Molly turned when she noticed the door open and was delighted to realize that it was all Ryan's doing. Every single person in that ward could barely deny that Ryan and Molly had eyes only for one another.

For the first time in his life, James was enthusiastically aware of how Ryan took his daughter's breath away, while Ryan's whole face lit up when he appeared in Molly's presence. Ryan slowly walked around to her, and smiled breathlessly at her, "Hey." He lovingly held her in his arms. "Hey yourself."

James stood in silence while scrutinizing Ryan and Molly from a distance. At that very moment, he wholly understood what it was about Ryan and Molly that he could never make sense of. It was by no means plain and simply love, and it was in no way measly affection, their souls had come together as it should have, and was undoubtedly imperative for one another to continue to survive. They had come from one, a flame that was split in two. He had made the biggest mistake of his entire life when he sought to divide them. Molly never, not at all belonged to Sue and James, not even for a moment. From the second she was brought into this crooked world, she belonged to Ryan. The manner in which their lives had turned out at that very instant, was unerringly the way it was intended to, long before they were even born. He was severely distressed to discover that he had stolen time from them, but he was enormously comforted by the fact that Molly had found her way back home to Ryan. With tears of delight and pleasure he softly whispered, "That's Ryan's girl."

With love,

Ryan & Molly

Thank you for sharing our story with us.

Goodnight.

Alice VL